☆

BILL COLES

The Spare Heir Handbook

☆

PRINCE
HARRY'S
VERY BEST
TIPS FOR THE
ROYAL BABY

With a special foreword by
'HRH Prince Andrew'

☆

Legend Press Ltd, The Old Fire Station,
140 Tabernacle Street, London, EC2A 4SD
info@legend-paperbooks.co.uk
www.legendtimesgroup.co.uk / @legend_press

Print ISBN 978-1-7850798-8-7
Ebook ISBN 978-1-7850798-9-4

Set in Times. Printed in the United Kingdom by Clays Ltd.
Cover design by Gudrun Jobst www.yotedesign.com
Front cover illustration by Alan McGowan

'A superbly crafted memoir.'
Daily Express

'Try *Dave Cameron's Schooldays* for jolly
fictional japes. It helps to explain the real Dave's
determination to whip us into shape.'
Edwina Currie, *The Times*

'A beautiful book, managing to use a simple narrative
voice without consequently bland style – honesty,
beauty, and passion pervade the novel but so do
humour, youthfulness and energy.'
Stuck in a Book

'My own piano teacher was called Mr Bagston and
frankly I don't think any power on earth could have
persuaded us to create a scene of the kind Coles so
movingly describes!'
Boris Johnson, *London Mayor*

'Passionate and excrutiatingly compelling.'
Curledup.com

'A piece of glorious effrontery... takes an honourable
place amid the ranks of lampoons.'
The Herald

'Compellingly vivid, the most sustained description of
apocalypse since Robert Harris's *Pompeii*.'
The Financial Times

Also by Bill Coles

Dave Cameron's Schooldays (Legend Press)
Simon Cowell: The Sex Factor (Legend Press)
Red Top, Being a Reporter: Ethically, Legally and with Panache (Paperbooks)

Also by William Coles

The Well-Tempered Clavier (Legend Press)
Lord Lucan: My Story (Legend Press)
Mr Two-Bomb (Legend Press)
The Woman Who Made Men Cry
(Thames River Press)
The Woman Who Knew What She Wanted
(Thames River Press)
The Woman Who Was The Desert Dream
(Thames River Press)
The Woman Who Dared to Dare
(Thames River Press)

To the One True King (of Satire), Giles Pilbrow

TABLE of CONTENTS

✩ ✩ ✩ ✩ ✩ ✩ ✩ ✩ ✩ ✩

*From one Spare Heir
to another,*

*To my darling niece, wishing
you all of my love, from your
doting Uncle Harry.*

*And to all those other Spare
Heirs in the world, forever
having to play catch-up behind
their big brothers and their big
sisters, I also have something
to say: please, please, please,
do what I say, NOT what I
do.*

*I know all the theory of what
a Spare ought to be doing.
I'm just not so hot on the
practice.*

Big kisses,

Harry X

✩ ✩ ✩ ✩ ✩ ✩ ✩ ✩ ✩ ✩

Foreword by His Royal Highness
Prince Andrew

If I hadn't been so bally lazy, I'd have written this book thirty years ago – when it was me who was the Spare Heir and when it was Prince Harry who was demoting me down the Royal line of succession.

But even if I hadn't been so bally lazy, I still couldn't have written this book, because… I can't bloody well write!

So hats off to Harry for knuckling under to produce this long overdue guide for junior Royals. I've had a flick through and it appears to be a sort of how-to manual for the younger brothers and sisters of the Heir to the Throne. Packed with top tips, or so I'm told, and just the sort of book that I could have done with myself fifty years ago. Not that it would have done me much good as I was never much of a reader.

When young Harry asked me to write the foreword for this book, he told me to say that it's a jolly good read, that it would be most beneficial to every younger brother and sister on earth, and that therefore and in consequence, please buy this book and give it to all your friends.

Without further ado: please buy this book
and give it to all your friends. It's a jolly
good read and younger brothers and sisters
everywhere will find it most beneficial.

I thank you!

HRH Prince Andrew

P.S. I never did it.
Never! Not me! Not ever!

THE SPARE HEIR FANTASY

☆

So here, darling Charlotte, and all those other darling Spares, is thirty years of wisdom. Thirty years of Royal cock-ups. If you can dodge even a few of my prat-falls, then you will avoid a heap of embarrassment. It's not the personal embarrassment. I'm fine with that. It's shaming your mum and your dad and your grannies and your grandads. That's much harder to deal with.

Now I know that I'm a Prince and a 'His Royal Highness', so there will be a lot of Spares out there wondering just what on earth this book has got to do with them.

I'll tell you.

I may have been born with a silver spoon in my mouth. But I also know what it's like to spend your every waking day playing second fiddle to the Number One. To the Heir. To the kid who's going to wear the crown. **I, more than anyone else on this earth, know what it's like to be the Spare, just waiting, waiting, waiting, for that day, which is never going to happen, when they're going to drop off the perch.**

But they never do.   ☆

Or at least: they very rarely do.

Half a lifetime ago, we had gathered at Buckingham Palace. Cousins, uncles, aunts, the first-rate Royals, the third-rate Royals – we were all there. We'd had a lunch, unbelievably stiff, and then we were due to go out onto the Palace balcony to wave at the tens of thousands of people waiting for us on the Mall. There was going to be a fly-past.

The first time you do the Royal wave, it's quite fun.

Second time, it's still quite fun.

But by the time you've done it 1,000 times it gets pretty dull. I don't know how you feel after you've done it 20,000 times like Granny – that'd be once a day, every day, for 60 years. Maybe you are so numbed that you don't even notice it.

Thousands of smiling strangers waving their flags and all they ever want you to do is wave back at them. They are like the kids who wave at the steam trains, and the Royals... the Royals are little better than zoo animals.

So after our formal lunch, we drift up to the balcony room. The door is finally opened and one by one we go out onto the balcony, stragglers to the side, players to the middle.

That was the first time that I didn't have the stomach for it. What was the point? Going out onto the balcony and waving and waving – and for what? It seemed so utterly meaningless.

At the last minute, I ducked out of going onto the balcony. I said I had a dodgy stomach. I went to the lavatory.

I was having a quiet fag, thinking about not very much at all, when I heard the rumble of the planes on the fly-past. Red Arrows, Spitfires, helicopters, bombers.

And it was then that, for the first time, I allowed my

imagination to run riot.

What if…

What if… the pilot of one of the Lancaster bombers had a heart attack?

What if… that stricken bomber just happened to nose-dive straight towards the ground?

Or… nose-dive straight into the Buckingham Palace balcony?

All the Royals dead.

All the Heirs dead.

And with one single bound…

The Spare Heir comes into his own!

I think you know what I'm thinking. We are talking about nothing less than: King Harry The Ninth.

Just an idle daydream.

I remember smirking to myself in the mirror.

I stubbed out my cigarette and skulked out to join the others and Grandad farted, just like he loves to do when we are all together on the balcony, and we all laughed, and it was good to be alive. The Heir was still there, and I was still the Spare Heir going nowhere fast.

And the point of this all being… there are a lot of Spares out there who dream of this far-off, probably never-going-to-happen day when they might become the genuine Heir. I, also, have had these thoughts – like that minute of daydreaming in the Palace lavatory.

But other Spares… they fritter away years of their lives hungering after this mirage. Some of them seriously imagine that everything will be just perfect if the Heir dies, and if they get moved up to the top slot.

This is not the way to lead your life. There is no

happiness to be found if you follow this path.

First of all – it's probably not going to happen. In all likelihood, you will be the Spare Heir till the end of your days. In fact – as has happened to me – you may even get knocked a few pegs down the perch as your big brother George has Heirs and Spares of his own.

What I'm saying is: do not pin your hopes on something that is as fanciful as the crock of gold at the end of the rainbow. And just by the by, even if you do get your hands on that crock of gold, it will only ever turn out to be a crock of shite.

So – this is what you need to know. When you're a Spare, there are up-sides, there are down-sides. As in life. You may not be getting the big house or the land or the title. But what you WILL be getting is something much, much more valuable. You'll have the freedom to do… whatever it is that you want to do. Think your dad Prince Billy can do that? No – he and your mother Kate are stuck in this glorious gilded cage until the day they die.

Me, on the other hand? I do also live in a bit of a cage. It's quite a nice cage, but it is a cage nonetheless with a paparazzo stalker waiting for me just outside the front door. But what I do know is that I've got a hell of a sight more freedom than if I were Heir Number One.

So live your life in the here and now. Accept the cards that you've been dealt.

Do not waste one single second of your days dreaming about this wonderful far-off day when you might become the Number One Heir. It's probably never going to happen. And even if it does, dreaming

18

about it won't make it come any quicker. If you're dreaming about being the Heir, then you'll never actually be living in the moment.

Even when you are the Heir, you might still have to wait one hell of a long time before you ever get to run the train-set. Look at my dad! He'll be in his seventies before he ever gets his hands on the crown! While most people are thinking about retirement, he'll still be hanging on in there for the day when he becomes Charles III.

I'm not saying that dreaming can't be fun.

But do not let it take over your life. Do not think, even for a moment, about 'how much better' your life might be if it was you who'd got the top slot.

That is the path to madness and to misery. ☆

There are a lot of perks to being a Spare. These are perks without (much) responsibility. So don't ever dwell on what might have been – or what might be yet to come. You stick to the moment. You don't whine. And you make the most of what you've damn well been given.

FAMILY

VERY USEFUL FACT #1
I never leave home without a tin of Spam – and a
bottle of Tabasco.
A Spare Heir gets to eat a lot of bland food
on what we call The Rubber Chicken Circuit. The
Tabasco peps it up.
Works pretty much anywhere – except the Arctic.
Just freezes solid.
A Tabasco ice-lolly?
That'd make your eyes water!

BORN TO BE RUDE

Your daddy, Big Bruv Billy, was having one of his bad days. He can get a bit like that. Just turns into a bit of a sour-puss. I think he was moaning about his bloody hair.

Guess what – the stuff is falling out. Well, sometimes it happens to guys in their thirties. It's not great, but, as the Monty Python team tell us, it's not the **Spanish Inquisition**.

Billy has got a bit of a problem with his hair in that, unlike any other bloke, he can't do anything about it. He can't go and get his bald pate re-thatched with hairs that have been tweezered from his bum – and he certainly can't wear a wig. He'd just look vain and ridiculous.

So he's got to soak it up, and he does it with pretty good grace – makes little quips about your brother, George, having more hair than he does.

He's not trying to hide it either – no combover for Billy, and instead his thinning hair is all trimmed nice and short. He's got a big bald patch and he's proud of it! (In fact it's more than a 'patch'. He's currently at that halfway house stage between a 'bald patch' and 'bald as an egg'.)

Not that you'd ever guess, but it does rather get him down.

And that's where the Spare comes in.

The Spare's job is not just to think the unthinkable,

23

but to say the unsayable.

One morning I caught him in the bathroom. He'd got a couple of mirrors fixed up so that he could inspect his bald patch – and, just the same as usual, it was pretty big and it was getting bigger.

Billy looked up and scowled. He started to rub in one of those hair potions. Not that it was going to do him a blind bit of good, as he's been trying those potions for years now.

'Cheer up chicken!' I said. 'You'll be making history with that bald head of yours.'

He looks at me. World-weary.

'Why will I make history?' he says.

'Look mate – you'll be the first bald British King that there's ever been! That's something to be pretty proud of, isn't it?'

'I'm sure that at least half of the kings were bald,' he says, stroppy-like.

'But they all wore wigs,' I said. 'So nobody's got any idea if they had hair or not. You, on the other hand – you won't be wearing a wig.'

Billy looks at himself in the mirror. Spaniel eyes. One of his soulful stares. 'I'll be the first bald monarch in history.'

'Probably not the first monarch,' I said. 'Wasn't old Elizabeth a baldicoot?'

'Do you have to use the word baldicoot?'

'Here's a thought. When they do your face for the stamps and all the coins, you might be better off wearing your crown.'

'To hide the fact that I'll have no hair.'

'Exactly!' I cackled. "Just think how they'll remember you in hundreds of years time! You'll be doing all these great things, running all these wonderful charities, putting in a really solid turn as King – and yet how will they remember you?'

'How will they remember me?'

'You'll be known as Billy the Baldy!'

He stares at me – looking rather like a peevish dormouse that's been disturbed in the middle of breakfast. 'Billy the Baldy? Where the hell did that come from?'

'The Press has been using it for ages,' I said. 'Ever since I coined the name two years ago.'

'You made that name up?'

'No need to thank me.'

I was about to leave the bathroom when I noticed a hairbrush by the sink. It was ivory-backed, rather fine. 'You won't be needing this for much longer,' I said. 'Can I have it?'

Getting the drift? One of your main roles as a Spare is to be a short, bracing slap-in-the-face to your big brother. The Heirs spend their entire lives surrounded by boot-lickers and Yes-Sirring flunkies. Their world is filled with grovelling toad-eaters.

The Spare is the antidote.

You are the one person who can say whatever the hell you like – and, preferably, the ruder the better.

(Obviously you've got to say it to their face. Mocking them in public can work but it's risky.)

TOP PRINCE HARRY JOKES: #2

Although a few people know of Prince William's ball control skills, the whole world knows about Prince Harry's tackle.

WHO'S THE DADDY? ☆

You might not believe it, but I am actually aware of all these rumours that have been floating around for the past three decades that my dad might not be… my dad.

It has been suggested that my real father might in fact be a certain ginger scoundrel. An enormously well-endowed ginger scoundrel who occasionally used to go by the name of (Wee Willy) 'Winkie' and who had a brain the size of a pea.

I've seen it in the papers – read it in books. It sometimes crops up on TV, masquerading as some quirky sitcom sub-plot where a maid is trying to collect some of my DNA. (Hair, toenails and other such things.)

Then, very, very occasionally, a certain ginger scoundrel has found himself so strapped for cash that he has taken it upon himself to go to the Press and call for a DNA test so that we can prove 'once and for all' just who's the daddy.

Well…

I remember once hearing one of the Palace Press officers deal with a truly insane Press query from America. The question was something like, 'Isn't it outrageous that the Queen owns all these empty Palaces around Britain when they could be turned into holiday lets?'

The Press Officer breathes in.

She pauses.

And she says: **'Well it's a view.'**

I love that!

'It's a view!' (As in – you're more than entitled

to your opinion, crappy or otherwise, but I will not be dignifying it with a comment. It's a view!)

So when people come to me with all these weird theories about a certain ginger scoundrel, I just say…
It's a view.

However. This is my view. (And I know this may sound a little ironic given that I'm a Royal Spare, and considering the fact that the entire basis of the Royal family is our blood-line…)

But nevertheless…

The people who make up our family are not necessarily the people who have any blood ties with us. Our family is very simply made up of the people who've made time for us. A man may be your biological father; but your real father is the man who's brought you up, who's spent time with you, who's given you your values.

And the same goes with uncles and aunts and cousins. These people may share some ancestors with you, but whether they're your real family – whether you want to spend time with them – depends on how you get on with them. How much time they've spent with you. Whether you can trust them or whether they'll sell you down the Swanee the first chance they get.

You only have one dad – and that is the guy who put in the hours with you when you were a kid. Ginger-haired scoundrels need not apply.

First day at Eton, thirteen years old, very, very nervy. We sit down for tea, it's all very forced, and I'm meeting these nine other new boys who, for better or worse, I am going to be living with for the next five years. Five years! You're going to get pretty cosy with each other after five years!

And of course some you like, and some you don't like so much. But here's the thing.

If you're at a boarding school, then you're going to be rubbing shoulders with your housemates for quite a long time.

So you make it work.

There might be the occasional scrap.

But generally, you learn to live with each other.

It's the same with the Royal family.

And it's the same – or so Billy tells me – with your in-laws.

In your life, you're going to be seeing a whole load of these people. In the Royal family, even the most far-flung relations are still family, so at least twice a year, we all get together – cousins and second cousins and cousins twice removed.

The Royals, however, have this weird pecking order. The top dogs are not necessarily the oldest people or the most venerable, or the people who've done something worthwhile with their lives.

No – the top dogs are the ones who, in essence, are in the top tier of the line of succession.

I used to be a top dog – but now, thanks to George and you, and any other siblings that you might have, I am being knocked ever further down the top table.

Don't get me wrong, I am so happy about that.

But anyway – what I'm saying is that if you're going to be seeing people twice a year, every year, for the rest of your entire goddamn life, then it's probably just as well to get on with them.

Not worth having rows. Not worth having a feud which rumbles on from one year to the next.

For instance.

Your dad had just started at St Andrews University, and for a couple of days the paparazzi had a free-for-all. They were allowed to take all the pictures they wanted.

And then after a couple of days, all the photographers – God rot them – were sent packing with a flea in their ear.

And off they all went.

All save for a certain film crew from a certain London-based film company, which just happened to be run by Uncle Eddie.

Some phone calls were made.

The film crew was sent packing.

But it wasn't worth having a row over. I mean, Eddie is a bit of a clown. But he's also just another Spare Heir like me – and like you – and so he's just doing the best he can to find some purpose to being a Prince.

☆  ☆

At Eton, big bruv Billy was a useful runner.

One crisp winter's afternoon, it was the school steeplechase. Six or seven miles, I guess, through the mud and the fields of Eton and Datchet.

I had it all planned.

Straight after lunch, I got on my bike and pedalled off out on the steeplechase route.

About four or five miles out, I parked up and hid behind a tree.

Spying through the ivy, I could see this long line of runners in the distance – and there, right up with the front-runners, was Billy. He's red in the face, blowing like an old carthorse. I could hear him from fifty yards away.

He's just running past when I jump out from my hiding place. 'Can I have your autograph?' I shouted.

Gave him such a shock he fell into the mud.

A stream of runners scampered past.

Billy sat in the mud bawling me out.

Everything was exactly as it should be.

There is a lot of people out there who imagine the primary role of a Spare is to step up to the plate if the Heir chokes on a tomato and drops down dead.

Stuff and nonsense!

It's never going to happen. Even if it is going to happen, there's diddly-squat you can do about it.

Forget about it!

The main thing you're supposed to be doing as the Spare is this: **taking the bloody piss.**

Your main purpose as a Royal is to keep your big brother George honest. Stop the little blighter getting too above himself.

It's your job to prick the bubble. To make sure he doesn't get too cocksure – too up himself.

The Spare's job is to stop the Heir's head from getting too bloody big. **Simple as that.**

You are the court jester!

There are any number of ways that you could bring the Heir down a peg.

Practical jokes. We love practical jokes! Prank them in the bedroom – in the lavatory. Prank the Heir when they're out having a run. When they're having their first date. When they're off to some 'extremely important' Royal reception.

Prank hard and prank often!

Prince Billy's not too bad, actually.

But there are a number of Royals around who take themselves far too seriously.

These are the people who can be completely suckered with a practical joke. They take themselves so seriously that it just doesn't even cross their minds that they might be on the receiving end of a prank.

Other ways.

At some stage in his life, the Heir is going to make a dickhead of himself.

Might be with a lover.

Might be on holiday.

Might be on his first day at work.

It's the Spare's job to tell him he's behaving like a moron! Nobody else is going to – because the Palace is stuffed to the gunnels with crawlers and toadies and slime-ball sycophants who are obsessed by positions and titles. What they don't understand is that the Heir may be a Prince – but he's still a guy and he's still going to cock things up. Probably more likely to cock things up.

We Spares are there for the cock-ups. We love it. We tease them. We prank them. We put them right back in their box.

This is what we were born to do.

Keeping the Spare Honest

If I'd had any brains, I'd have sniffed out there was something very, very wrong with the invitation.

It was an invite to Harry Meade's 22nd birthday – stiff card, engraved, gilt edging, the works.

And the theme of Harry's party was going to be: Native and Colonial.

Alarm bells!

Right from the start, it was going to put a lot of people's noses out of joint.

But as I may have mentioned.

I don't really think things through.

Just do what seems best at the time.

And as for the consequences…

Stuff 'em!

It was early 2005, and I'd been due to start at Sandhurst in the spring, but unfortunately I'd injured my bloody knee while teaching some kids how to play rugby.

Left me with a bit of time on my hands.

And what does the devil find for loafing louts who are idling the hours away?

He finds work for them!

I was staying at Highgrove, the old man's house in Gloucestershire. Not much going on. I went off to have a browse in the local fancy-dress shop, Maud's Cotswold Costumes.

Maud had hundreds of outfits – animals, monsters, witches, superheroes. You name it, Maud had it.

I reckon if I had chosen any other outfit than the one I picked – any outfit at all – then nobody would have heard a thing about Harry Meade's bloody birthday party.

But as it was...

I wandered round and round Maud's shop and found myself increasingly drawn to a sandy-coloured uniform. I liked it. It matched my hair.

A Nazi uniform, complete with Swastika armband.

Don't know what it is about the Nazis, but young men are fascinated by them. I certainly was. The Nazis are the world's most terrifying bogeymen.

They're monsters.

But, particularly for young, doltish Princes who are obsessed by all things military, bizarrely, the Nazis do have an allure.

Can't really explain it. ☆

But it's there.

I dress up in my Nazi uniform and I go to the party.

Guy Bloody Pelly dresses up as my granny, The Queen! The nerve of him!

And – as sure as eggs is eggs – some grease-monkey gets a snap of me in my uniform, and then three days later it's all over the front page of *The Sun*.

My bad.
My very, very bad.

I'm not whining about being snapped at a private party. It is how it is.

But I could have done with somebody – like an

33

older brother, say, or a mate – who could have given me a nudge. Who could have whispered in my ear: 'Not a good idea'.

Would have saved me a whole heap of hassle.

Heirs need someone to give it to them straight. That's your job.

Spares also need someone to keep them straight. That's not necessarily going to be the Heir. But it's somebody who has a sound head on their shoulders.

It's up to you to find that guy.
And then listen to what he says.
Especially when he's telling you something
you don't want to hear.

TOP PRINCE HARRY JOKES: #3

I completely understand why Prince Harry
dressed as a Nazi.
I mean we all have a bad Heir day once in a while.

PIPPA'S ARSE

When Billy was getting married to your mum, I remember the first time I clocked your Auntie Pippa's arse. Now, it might seem weird me talking about your aunt like that, but bear with me. Skin-tight white silk dress. Clingy. Not a dimple in sight. Like a perfect Cox's Orange Pippin.

I complimented Pippa after the wedding, when we were on the balcony waiting for Billy to kiss your mum.

'Nice bum,' I said.

'Thanks,' she said. 'I worked my ass off.'

And didn't it just pay off?

My point being? While everyone is off making a hoo-ha about your aunt's bum, at the end of the day, they're family. **And if you can't make a joke at your family's expense, then what can you joke about?**

While I'm on the subject...

A lot of people out there are wondering just why Pippa and I never got it together.

I mean there you've got Pippa: smoking hot, available, desperate to bag her own title.

And there you've got me: HRH Prince Horny Goat.

Don't know what happened between Pippa and me.

Gave it a shot.

Felt – I guess – like trying to cop a feel off your mum's sister.

She certainly had the arse. But the chemistry just wasn't there.

You've either got it or you ain't, but if it's not there, then there's no faking it.　　　　　　☆

TOP PRINCE HARRY JOKES: #4

Just seen those Prince Harry pictures.
Step aside Pippa. That's a proper Royal arse.

MILLIONAIRE A-HOLES

Masked balls are great because you're wearing, well, a mask.

This means it is much easier to be anonymous. Instead of just being HRH Prince Harry who must be called Sir at all times, you are merely another punter who like every other party-goer has to sing for his supper.

You have to rely solely on the quality of your banter. And on chemistry.

On the other hand... there are some people, the rich egomaniac dick-heads, who don't enjoy masked balls. They don't like not being recognised. They'd rather you knew who they were so you could get into the dust and grovel.

Whereupon...   ☆

A masked ball at some pile outside London and I am dressed as Zorro, all in black, from my cape to my black cowboy boots, while hanging from my belt is a sword, a genuine sword, a foil. To get into the part, I'd even stuck a black moustache onto my top lip. Verrry dashing.

With my face mask and the black kerchief round my head, I could have been anybody.

Or nobody.

The women at masked balls have a slightly different remit from the men. They've got to wear a mask, because otherwise they'd be kill-joys.

But nevertheless... they do not like to hide their light under a bushel. If they're smoking hot, then they want the other guests to know it.

This is fantastic for guys like me because though the women may be masked, the gorgeous ones still stand out. We make a beeline for them. We chat them up and, we have to stand or fall on the quality of our repartee.

While I was getting a drink, I had spied a very tall

blonde woman who was dressed as a peacock. That's quite a big clue. If a woman has taken the effort to dress up as a peacock, then they're probably a bit of a peacock.

I picked up two glasses of Champagne and sidled over to the peacock. 'Are you a peacock or a bird of paradise?' I asked.

'I'm a peahen,' she said.

'But with a peacock's feathers.'

'It's a shame that the peahens are so dowdy.' She accepted the glass of Champagne. 'I hoped that at a masked ball we might be allowed some artistic licence.'

'We'll have to see if your outfit is approved by the Masked Ball Committee.'

Touché!

'And who are you then?' she asked, perhaps a little nettled.

'Who do you think I am?'

'Are you Black Beauty?'

'Very good try, but no.'

A finger strays to her pretty red lips. 'Are you perhaps Dick Turpin?'

'Another excellent try, but no.'

'Are you the Man in Black?'

'No.'   ☆

'The Milk Tray man?'

'No.'   ☆

'James Bond?'

'From the Roger Moore era? Close, but no.'

'Are you... '

I am enjoying myself. Neither of us has a clue who the other one is, and we are just juggling with words.

Before my beautiful peahen can say another

word, we are joined by another guest. He is arrayed in yellow silk with a swathe of jewels across his chest; he's got a turban on, along with a very small silver mask. I guess he's trying to be a Sultan.

I'm pretty sure I know who he is. And that's because he wants to be recognised.

The Sultan had made his millions by pumping out shite TV programmes. For the sake of this story, he is going to need a name, so let's call him... **Simon.**

Simon sidles up next to us. 'All right gorgeous, how're you?' he says.

'Very well,' she says. 'And how are you?'

'Oh I'm good,' he purrs. He's only really talking to the peahen, hasn't even bothered to look at me. 'I'm very, very good.'

'So shall we guess who you've come as?' says the peahen.

'If you like,' he says. He's twinkling, as if he knows something we don't. The thing is though – we already know. He's a big fat multi-millionaire with all the charm of a turd.

'Have you come as a corn on the cob?' I say.

'Err – no,' he says, as if he's talking to a particularly dim-witted guest. For the first time he turns his dull eyes on me. Not interested.

The peahen pipes up. Simon is much more interested in the peahen. 'Are you a genie?' she says.

'Popped up from Aladdin's lamp?' says Simon. 'No – I'm afraid not.'

'Are you a human goldfish?' I ask.

By now, the message is beginning to seep through. We couldn't care less who Simon is – we're just taking the mickey.

'Very funny,' he says. Very fixed smile.

'I'm not totally sure,' says the peahen, 'but I think I might have got it. Are you… are you a human streak of piss?'

The fixed smile drops.

He utters the immortal words: **'Do you know who I am?'**

'That's exactly what we're trying to work out,' I say. 'All yellow silk. Are you a canary? Are you one of the stars of Norwich City?'

'I think you're a human humbug,' says the peahen.

'I used to love humbugs!' I said. 'Haven't had one of those in years.'

'I've always wondered why Scrooge was for ever saying Bah Humbug,' says the beautiful peahen. 'I mean why humbugs? Were they his favourite sweet?'

Simon is now looking thoroughly pissed off. He doesn't know what to do! He is so up his own backside that he is incapable of larking around.

'Scrooge would have sounded much better if he'd said, "Bah Maltesers,"' I said.

The peahen titters. I wanted to kiss her. Hadn't even see her face and in under five minutes I'm already a little in love with her – and just because we were having a laugh with each other.

'Bah Mars Bars!' she said.

'Bah Rowntrees Fruit Pastilles!'

'Bah marshmallow!'

It's nothing much, but we are howling with laughter and Simon's fixed smile is only making us laugh even harder.

The peahen and I carry on riffing for a while and Simon starts to pout, before eventually he utters, again, 'Do you know who I am?'

'I thought we'd already been over this one,' I said. 'Are you Bananaman?'

And the peahen strikes: 'You look like that smug TV mogul, Simon What'sisname. God a what a bore he is!'

Simon's smile becomes just that little bit more fixed.

'Do you know who I am?' I said.

'Who are you?' says the peahen.

'I'm a gatecrasher,' I said. 'Came as one of the waiters. Slipped on my mask and here I am!'

Simon turns to go. The peahen roars.

One of the best nights of my life. And the best nights are usually the ones when I'm not a Prince.

In my line of work, I come across all sorts. I especially come across millionaires. They give money to charities. They buy seats at top tables. They secrete their way into that Seventh Circle of Hell, the Royal Circle, in the hope of sucking up some of our star dust.

What I know is that most multi-millionaires are arseholes.

They may be very good at making money. But this does not in any way mean that they are very good at being human beings.

If you're a control freak micro-manager who is ever-hungry for the next deal, you can make a ton of money... and also be a total dickhead.

These people love to surround themselves with **crawlers** who hang on their every word.

The incredible thing is how many crawlers there are. Just the thought of all this lovely money turns a lot of people into slobbering toadies.

If you suck up to a millionaire, then you might fondly imagine you'll see a slice of the action. But you won't actually see one bit of it! In my experience, millionaires are as tight as a gnat's chuff. They won't even buy you a drink, let alone take you on holiday.

So there the millionaires sit, holding court as they dole out their worldly wisdom – and you're damn well expected to listen because they've got a lot of money.

But outside their tiny, tiny worlds, they know absolutely nothing. They are bolshy, highly-strung airheads.

Just because somebody's rich, it doesn't mean they're worth talking to.

My advice: steer clear of them. And steer clear of the crawlers.

DATING

VERY USEFUL FACT #2

As the Royal Spare, you will be one of the most photographed people on the planet.

This rather means that you can't do too much fiddling with your looks. Can't really have botox. Can't have a facelift. Certainly can't have a hair transplant.

If you're a Spare, you're basically stuck with the looks you've got.

But it doesn't matter what you look like. Even if you have the face of a frog, there will still be millions of people out there throwing themselves at you. Just look at Prince Albert of Monaco!

 Lovers

All my life, for as long as I can remember, I have been very interested in girls. Don't really understand them, mind – don't know what it is that makes these exotic creatures tick. But I adore women.

One day when I was about fifteen, we were spending Christmas at Balmoral. You may have heard of the place. The old man knocked on my bedroom door and shuffled into my room.

We started talking about the next day's shooting, though it was all a little awkward. I sensed that the old man had something to tell me.

There was a lull in the conversation and then at length he got to the matter in hand: my virginity.

There was a lot of hemming and hawing.

There was a lot of tugging at his throat as he stared out of the window.

This is what he told me.

And this is what I am now telling you.

In fifteen years' time, I am sure you will be utterly gorgeous. You may even be charming and considerate and sweet-natured.

You may be all of that – or you may in fact be a total minger with all the manners of a rabid jackal.

But I tell you what – it won't make a blind bit of difference, because even if you're the most foul-mouthed slapper that ever walked this earth, there are still going to be THOUSANDS AND THOUSANDS of people who are going to want to sleep with you.

That's because you're a Spare! That's because you're a blue-blood! That's because one day your daddy's going to be King!

And the great joy of being a Spare is that you can sleep with as many of these people as you like. Royal Spares are almost expected to go out and sow their oats.

But.

And it's a big But.

Don't you go getting yourself knocked up!

Just like my dear old dad told me all those years ago, you can sleep with whoever you like. Within reason, you can notch up quite a fair number of lovers. (More tricky to continue playing the field when you're married but obviously not impossible.)

No-one's going to be complaining about that. We're in the 21st century!

But – at least for a Royal Spare – having babies out of wedlock is still a no-no.

So in practical terms, what does this all mean? (I can still see the old man going tomato red with embarrassment as he painfully explained this to me.)

It means that, until you get to know your lovers very, very well, and until you can trust them, then you have to take responsibility for the contraception. Basically and in essence: at all times, you want to be careful. Getting my drift?

When you are older, you will be meeting stunning, versatile people who want to jump into bed with you. They will be telling you that it's all covered. Not to worry about a thing.

And most of the time they'll be telling the truth.

But some of the time, they won't. They may not be lying. But let's just say that they're being economical with the truth.

So until that happy day that you have complete and total confidence in your lover, you want to take it upon yourself to provide the protection. It's not that we don't trust these people. It's just that we don't trust people until... we know they can be trusted.

It's regrettable but it is true. There are thousands of people out there who would like nothing more than to have a kid with you after a one night stand. Kerrr-ching! All of the money! All of the fame! None of the responsibility! What's not to like?

It's not a good idea for young Royals to be having unplanned kids. For a Royal Spare, it's a complete disaster. One night of pleasure. Years and years – and years – of hassle.

FANTASY BOYS ☆

Let me tell you something that I have in common with David Beckham.

We both love women.

I really love women.

David perhaps loves women even more.

But just because we love women, that isn't going to stop blokes fancying us too.

Both of us are, in fact, gay icons. Gay men love us. And we love gay men. Though – at least speaking for myself – I haven't hopped into bed with any of them.

Yet.

Anyway – chances are that if you're a Royal, then a lot of people are going to find you very, very sexy. It's not that you will necessarily BE sexy. I ain't sexy.

But if you're having your picture slapped on the front pages of the papers and the glossies every other week, then you sort of worm your way into people's sexual fantasies. They don't fancy you. But after a while, they sort of start thinking to themselves: nice bit of trouser – I wonder what he'd be like in bed.

It is how it is. If you're the Spare Heir you will be featuring in a fair few people's fantasies. For a lot of people, you will be their ultimate fantasy.

And one day, doubtless, you will be making somebody's fantasies come true. They'll have been lusting after you for an absolute age – and then there you are, in the flesh.

The fantasy has come to life!

And let me tell you now: it is one complete and utter nightmare.

You will be doing yourself one immense favour if you can possibly, possibly avoid these fantasist nut-jobs.

I've done it a few times.

Won't ever go there again.

(All right – will endeavour not to ever go there again. You see the problem with a lot of these fantasists is that not only are they deranged but they also happen to be fantastically beautiful. A lethal combination. Lethal!)

But of course, despite all these magnificent pearls of wisdom from your old Uncle Harry, there will come the day when you DO go to bed with one of these fantasists who has been dreaming about bedding you every single night for perhaps the last five years. Maybe you're pissed. Maybe you fancy them. Maybe, maybe, maybe…

The point is you end up in bed with them.

Know what happens next?

48

Whatever you do – literally, whatever you do – they're going to end up disappointed. They've got this little fantasy going on in their heads and it is going to be just so perfect in every way.

And guess what? You're just a normal human being. You ain't perfect – in any way whatsoever. (Though you will, of course, always be perfect to me. And to your mum. And to your dad.)

So, this is wisdom speaking.

You will become a sexual icon for millions and millions of people, some of them gay and a whole load of them straight.

**Be very, very wary about sleeping
with these people.**

They are fantasists! By definition! And when they discover that the reality isn't shaping up to how they expected their fantasy to be, then they can go ever so slightly tonto.

THE TEST

When I was young and stupid, and when I didn't know the first thing about women, I used to shower my girlfriends with gifts.

They loved nothing more than being taken off on a five-star mini break.

I remember taking one girl – let's call her Pookie – off for a weekend to New York. First class flights. Unlimited Champagne. Staying at the Waldorf Astoria just by Central Park. The fanciest bars. A stroll over the road to buy Pookie some expensive trinket from Tiffany's.

I went the whole nine yards.

She showed her appreciation in the usual way.

We had a very pleasant time.

A few months later, we were staying up at Birkhall, the old man's place in Scotland. I'd planned a special surprise for her.

One morning before sunrise, I'd packed the Land Rover with everything you could possibly need for The Most Perfect Picnic On Earth. A fold-up table and two decent chairs; white tablecloth and (starched) napkins; crystal wine glasses and candles; bottle of fizz, bottle of white, bottle of red, bottle of brandy; side of smoked salmon, lemons, small loaf of bread; a leg of lamb and some couscous and salad.

I drove up into the hills, arrived at the most scenic spot I knew and unloaded the table and the two chairs. As for the rest of the gear, I left that all locked in the boot of the Land Rover. Got on my bike and tore back home to Birkhall in time to awake my darling Pookie with a kiss and cup of coffee.

We spent the rest of the morning messing around. After lunch I suggested going for a walk. Pookie pouted a bit. She really preferred shopping to walking, but after I'd told her that I had a surprise for her, she agreed to come. Perhaps she thought there would be some more jewellery at the end of it – maybe even an engagement ring.

We set off at about 4pm. I had a hip flask of whisky and a packet of Polos.

Perhaps I should have warned Pookie. She was wearing walking gear, as designed by somebody who's never set foot outside London.

First there were the midges. It was hot and muggy, barely a breath of wind, and the midges were out in force, biting every inch of naked flesh. After about two hours, Pookie was looking like she had a good dose of chicken pox.

Pookie started to moan. She took out her mirror to inspect her face and almost wept when she saw the blotches. Said she had some ball to go to in London.

The next thing: the heavens opened. Quite a storm, actually.

Welcome to Scotland.

We had a nip of whisky and a couple of Polos. We carried on plodding.

Somewhere along the way, I got lost. In the low cloud, one Scottish forest looks pretty much like another.

I tried finding out where we were on my mobile.

No dice.

Who ever would have thought it? You rarely get any mobile coverage in Scotland.

We soldier on.

By now, it's gone 8pm, Pookie is wet and her whining has ratcheted up into a full-on bellyache.

Through the mist, I recognise a particular cleft rock in the hills. Suddenly I know where we are.

We're back on track!

The belly-aching continues.

'Don't worry Pookie,' I coo. 'We'll be there soon. And when we get there, you'll just love it, I know you will.'

An hour later, the storm has petered out into a grey drizzle. We crest the top of the hill. The table and chairs are not quite how I left them. They've all been upended.

Maybe the wind turned them over.

And then I look around for the Land Rover.

No Land Rover.

I look at the table and on the ground I see empty bottles and various bits of food. They hadn't even bothered to slice the lamb, just gnawed it straight off the bone.

Having demolished our supper, those young scamps had driven off in the Land Rover.

If I could see those joyriders now, I would shake them by the hand and buy them a drink.

Though at the time, it did make for a **slightly** uncomfortable evening.

Pookie. Lets. Rip.

A whole load of effing and blinding. 'What do you mean – dragging me up to the top of this bloody hill?' she yelled. 'I'm cold and I'm hungry. How are we going to get back?'

Me: 'I'll see if I can call a car.'

Pookie: 'I am soaked!'

And then when she realised that my mobile (still) didn't have any coverage, Pookie started shrieking with rage. Quite an ear-bashing.

There was still a bit of meat on the lamb-bone so I pocketed that, and we started the long trudge back home. I offered Pookie a bite of meat but all she could do was complain about her blisters.

We finally got back to Birkhall at about midnight, though the complaining went on for a long time after that.

The next day I wake Pookie with her customary coffee. Her face does perhaps look a little lumpy from the midge bites, but nothing that wouldn't mend.

Pookie stretches for a mirror.

Far from having calmed down after a good night's

kip, she starts to weep with rage.

And the penny drops.

For the rest of the day, I solicitously looked after Pookie. The next morning I dropped her off at the station so that she could get back to her ball in London.

And that – thank God – was the end of Pookie and me.

Pookie was beautiful, high maintenance and she will doubtless make some guy a wonderful wife.

But she was never going to be right for me.

And I realised that on the night of my Birkhall picnic.

So, I'm not saying that fancy five-star mini breaks in New York can't be wonderful. They're fun. Every so often, it's nice to treat yourself.

But they're not a good way to find out if you've found your mate.

I don't know much, but I do know this: **what you're looking for with your life-partner is a trouper.** Somebody who will be there with you in the ditch when the bullets are whistling overhead. Somebody who is not going to be too fazed when things go wrong.

When the shit hits the fan – as it most assuredly will – your perfect partner will be someone who doesn't whinge and doesn't whine. They will take it on the chin. Ideally, they'll be laughing about it. Comedy is just tragedy combined with the passage of time – and in my book, the shorter that passage of time is, the better. We don't like whiners. We like· roughy-toughies with thick skins and a well-honed sense of the ridiculous.

If no-one's dead and no-one's in hospital, and if all you've really got to complain about is that you have been mildly inconvenienced, then you are still way ahead of the game.

Part of this business of being a human means that shit occasionally happens.

Doesn't matter if you are the most pampered Royal on earth, shit is still going to happen. It tastes disgusting. That is rather the nature of shit.

You've still got to swallow it all the same.

You want a partner who's going to be pretty good at swallowing it too.

Spas are nice enough. Flying off for a week in Mustique is a pleasant way to unwind. The thing is though, anyone can behave decently when they're surrounded by luxury. (Well most people can – you're going to come across some snotties who always want more.)

A much better test for any potential soulmate is to throw them a curveball. Give them something they hadn't expected. See how they react when things go wrong. See how they react when things go very badly wrong.

That is how you find out if you've gotten yourself a keeper.

THE HARRY HUNTERS ☆

☆

I used to get a fair bit of adulation when I was attending to my Royal duties in Britain.

Whenever I went on a Royal walkabout, grinning and chatting, there would always be a whole host of people who wanted to see me and shake my hand. A lot of them used to think of me as some modern-day saint, specially come down from heaven – and good luck to them!

I am quite used to this sort of behaviour in Britain. Slightly barmy, but there you go. It's all part of the turf when you're a Spare Heir. And then I went on my first tour of America.

And in America, this sort of nutty adulation soars to a whole new level.

They called them 'The Harry Hunters' – and these women would do just about anything to speak to me. It's what happens when your country has no Lords, no Dukes, no Earls and certainly no Princes. For a few of them, meeting a real life Prince is absolute catnip.

Kind of exciting the first time it happens.

Lot of pretty women in America.

Big smiles. Ever so friendly.

They will do just about anything they can to get you into bed.

It's all very flattering.

You try it once. You try it twice. Maybe you even try it three times.

Hopefully you will soon get bored.

Because if you keep on trying it, you will soon get burned.

Maybe as badly burned as my great-great-uncle, Edward VIII. He gave up his whole damn throne for an American!

Wallis Simpson, I'm told, had one bedroom party piece that she'd learned out in the Far East: the Chinese Trick. I don't know specifically what this involved – though God would I like to know! – but it must have been one hell of a trick.

Don't know why, but American women know bedroom tricks which would curl your hair and make your arse whistle.

Doesn't mean they're keepers though.

It just means they're smoking hot in bed.

There is a difference.

Be wary with beautiful people.

Men, women, whatever. But when you're with a beautiful American, then you want to be on a very high state of alert, the full Defcon One, nerves twitching for the very least sign of enemy action. But that's the thing about this sort of enemy action – it always comes with a kiss and a stroke of the thigh.

Take especial care with any American who might just possibly look as if they're under the age of thirty. In all probability, they'll be about fifteen years old, and you'll get put right through the wringer.

Look what's happened to Uncle Andy! Pictures of the original Spare Heir cuddling up to a teenager. Doesn't look great.

Oh. Dear.

CHELSY

- - - - - - - - - - - - - - - - - -
TOP PRINCE HARRY JOKES: #5

I hear that Prince Harry has split up with his
girlfriend of five years.
I know he's a Royal and all, but that's a bit young isn't it?
- - - - - - - - - - - - - - - - - -

I love Taylor Swift. Lovely girl. Great singer.
We're pals. Good pals.

But we're just friends – really, really good friends
– and nothing more than that.

Just haven't gone there.

Never have. Never will.

So help me God.

After Taylor had split up again from one of her on-off
boyfriends, she wrote this fantastic song – and the
main chorus line went like this: 'We are never, ever,
ever… getting back together.'

Like it?

Doesn't matter what happens. Doesn't matter
what you do or what you say.

Taylor Swift ain't getting back together with you
any time soon. In fact, probably… never, ever, ever.

Which neatly brings me onto that brilliant, vivacious,
utterly mesmerising creature that is: Chelsy Davy.

I first met her a decade ago. We were inseparable.
Imagine two electricity pylons clashing together in the
most enormous thunderstorm. Ba-ba-boom!

First time that both of us had ever really been in
love. You can't top it.

A year or two down the line, the gilt was starting to rub off. Things happen. Other people catch your eye. (Didn't help that Uncle Andy was forever telling me to sow my oats.)

If you've been with someone for more than eighteen months, they start to become part of the wallpaper. They're background news. They may be eye-popping beauties, but you're no longer really aware of their looks.

For instance: Buckingham Palace is awash with fantastic pictures. Tens of millions of pounds-worth of pictures on the walls. The Palace collection could grace any gallery in the world.

And yet when you actually live in the Palace, you couldn't give two hoots! They're just the pictures on the walls. You walk past them every day, but you never for a moment stop to take a proper look.

You just take it all for granted.

Just like with me and Chelsy.

After a few years with Chelsy, I decided to heed Uncle Andy's advice and go and sow some of those wild oats that he'd been banging on about. ('You'll regret it if you don't!' he'd hooted.)

I sowed some oats.

And Chelsy... well she presumably was doing some oat-sowing as well. We were both of us too discreet to ask.

You see, the thing about ex-lovers is that the very moment you split up, their sex appeal goes through the roof.

Happens within a matter of days.

You've had this lover for over two years and it's not that they've necessarily lost their looks, and it's not

58

that you're no longer attracted to them, but the truth is there are a lot of people out there who you find plenty more attractive. And those cute little habits that your lover has, the way they flick their hair... well after a short time these habits are no longer quite so cute, in fact they're just bloody irritating.

So you split up, and within a few days you're doubtless having a run-round with those other much more beautiful human beings. You're finding out if that grass really is any greener.

And then a few months later, you just happen to bump into your ex.

Who has somehow miraculously transformed herself into The Most Beautiful Woman On Earth! What's she done? Was it a new diet? A new exercise regime? I have no idea – but all I do know is that as soon as I'd seen Chelsy again, we were exactly back to how we were when we'd first met. I fancied her rotten.

And off we go down that sweet, seductive path which we have already been down many, many times before.

Intoxicating!

We're back in love!

Second time round it doesn't last quite so long. Second time, your lover's amazing beauty begins to fade after a few months. The cute habits are now more irritating than ever.

Split up.

Sow more wild oats.

Meet Chelsy again at some friend's party – and of course she's right back to being The Most Beautiful

Woman On The Planet. Funnier than ever, more sexy than ever, cute habits just cuter than a fluffy ickle rabbit in her snuggly-wuggly hutch.

On again. Off again! Those irritating habits are now really starting to get up your nose – and notwithstanding that you've still got plenty of wild oats to sow, and wasn't that waitress just giving you the eye...

Off again, On again. Off again. In ever-decreasing circles, each time more frenetic, like a boat being sucked down into the depths of a whirlpool, going faster and faster until it is smashed all to pieces on the wet rocks beneath.

Happily enough, Chelsy and I did manage to avoid a complete shipwreck.

But now that we've finally split up, and had a bit of breathing space, I can now make this most solemn of pledges: we are never, ever, ever... getting back together.

Well at least until the next time we see each other – but I am now doing my level best to steer clear of the bewitching, beguiling, be-beautiful Chelsy.

So, to conclude, your ex-lovers have an extraordinary power over you. The moment you have split with them, they become exponentially more beautiful.

Doesn't matter what I say though.

You'll still split up with them – and get back together with them, over and over again, until you've finally sated yourselves on each other.

If you want to split for keeps, you're best off leaving the country.

☆

☆ THE ERMINE CAGE

It's one hell of a career being in the Royal family.

Most Royals are born to it. You, I'm afraid, haven't got much option.

There are also those plucky few who, for better or worse, opt to marry into it.

My mum.

Your mum.

Fergie.

Sophie.

Camilla.

But just like the Eagles sang in 'Hotel California', you can check out any time you want – but you can never leave.

It's a job for life. Even if you divorce, abdicate or renounce all your Royal ties, the paps will still stalk you. You'll still be photographed when you're out on the streets.

It takes a very, very special person to sign up for that lifetime sentence of being an HRH.

So when it comes to picking your life-partner, you've got to find someone who loves you – as opposed to someone who wants a slice of being a Royal and all those wonderful trappings that they imagine are a part of it.

For some people, it's their ultimate fantasy to lead this pampered life of Royal luxury. And then they sign up and within the year they see their fantasies turn all to shit.

If you can, steer well clear of these people.

In the last ten years, I have dated a lot of terrific women. But not a single one of them has even been remotely tempted to join me in my ermine cage.

The Greatest Spare in History ☆

Who was the greatest Spare in history?
This is debatable. ☆

There might be an argument for Henry VIII – who was the Spare until his big brother Arthur bought the farm. Good old Harry. Funny to think that he was the last Harry ever to wear the crown. So what the hell did he do? He had six wives. Smashed the monasteries. Stuffed it to the Pope and founded the Church of England.

Perhaps – just possibly – the greatest Spare could have been George V (that'd be your great-great-great-grandfather), who only got the job after his big brother the Duke of Clarence died of pneumonia. Though George V is a bit of a stretch – the only thing he's really famous for is his collection of stamps.

For my money, the greatest Spare of all time is **your great-great-grandfather George VI**, the affable stutterer who never even dreamed he'd be getting the top job.

He's married, he's got a couple of daughters, he's got one hell of a stutter – and a bit of a temper too, by all accounts. But he's very much on the sidelines. It's his big brother David who is the star of the show.

David (that'd be Edward VIII) was the good-looking charmer. Had women flocking at his feet – as you do when you're the Heir.

And then, as you know, Edward VIII gives up the throne for crazy old Wallis Simpson – and I can tell you now, that marriage was no bed of roses.

While Edward VIII had been all for cosying up with the Nazis, George VI becomes King just as Britain is going to war.

Didn't leave London, but stuck it out through the Blitz when the Luftwaffe were bombing the hell out of the capital.

Helped that he had a great wife – that'd be your great-great-granny, the Queen Mum.

Life as a Spare is a lot easier if you pick the right partner.

And if you don't pick the right partner, you're going to have a fairly torrid time of things as the disintegration of your marriage is dissected in the most minute detail in the Press and on the internet.

☆

On Future Queens

Whether you are the Heir or the Spare, you can have yourself one ton of lovers. As I've said, lots and lots and lots of people will want to sleep with you.

Even Billy had quite a few girlfriends. Quite a good-looking lad your dad was.

Anyway, over the years, Billy would introduce me to all these various girlfriends, who were all, without exception, totally charming. They could not do enough for him.

And I was, of course, charming back.

Just like you'd expect me to be.

And then there was the first time I met Kate. That'd be Kate, the Duchess of Cambridge, your mum.

You see, right from the very outset, Kate had set her heart on marrying Prince Billy.

So that first meeting with me was going to be quite a big deal – because I'm Billy's only brother on earth (that we know of, though I daresay we might have some rogue half-siblings in America and probably Australia too.)

She was one hell of a beauty, but because I was a Prince, I definitely had the upper hand.

First time we met was at a club in London. Can't remember which one. I'd been there for three hours chugging down Champagne and Red Bull when Billy glides over and thumps me on the arm.

'Harry,' he says. 'I'd like you to meet Kate.'

Problem was, I was utterly wasted. I didn't know Billy was bringing his girlfriend. But anyway, even if I had known, then so what?

'Hi Kate,' I said, and then vomited into a Champagne bucket. I don't think Kate was spattered.

Much.

The smile drops from Kate's face as she stares at me. Not often, I guess, that a Prince vomits over you.

Billy is apologising on my behalf. My face is covered in drool and for some reason I start howling with laughter.

Billy and Kate leave.

No matter. What do I care? Kate had seemed nice enough, but give it a few weeks and Billy would have another girlfriend and Kate would be history.

Whereas in fact… far from being history, Kate was making history.

In a few years' time, I'll be the Duke of York and Kate will have leapt past me in the Royal pecking order. Well, she'll be Her Majesty The Queen. (Won't her mum be pleased!) I'll have to bow to her!

Tricky to top that one, I tell you.

This is what I know.

The Heir, if they're anything like any of the other Heirs in history, is going to have lots and lots of lovers.

Almost all of them will fade from view. You might occasionally see them in the papers where they will always be referred to as 'an ex-Royal girlfriend'.

Except…

Except one is going to be The Keeper.

The Heir is eventually going to have to settle down. If she plays her cards right, that girlfriend will eventually become Queen.

Which very roughly means you don't want to piss off your brother's girlfriends.

Because one of them is going to be The Top Dog.

And if, on your first meeting, you happen to vomit all over her high-heeled Louboutins then she'll never let you forget it.

Always, always keep the girlfriends sweet. Be polite to them. Be interested. Be engaged. Because one day, one of these women is going to become the Queen, and if you haven't been sucking up to her right from the start, then she will mightily enjoy putting you back in your box.

VERY USEFUL FACT #3

When I go to a party, I like to create a good vibe. I like to let people know that the Party Prince has arrived. How do I do this?
I take off my shirt. Whirl it round my head. Shriek and toss my shirt across the room.
Once the Royal Spare goes topless, the party can really kick off. I'm not sure if this is good advice. Just something that works for me.

☆ ON FRIENDS

I couldn't put my finger on why my art teacher was giving me the creeps.

She was nice and smiley and affectionate – and she was very, very keen to help me out with my coursework. And I was only too happy to let her. I used to quite like painting when I was at school, but if a friendly teacher wanted to help me out with my work, I certainly wasn't going to tell them to back off.

And yet...

There was something about this woman that was fake.

At the time, I couldn't see it. I couldn't pin it down. **But beyond a doubt, I knew that something wasn't quite right.**

Anyway – I continued with my paintings, let her touch up the pictures in any way that she saw fit, and at the end of it all, I got a nice B grade in my A-level which was enough to get me into the army, and that was the end of it.

Although it wasn't quite the end of it.

How was I to know that she'd been tape-recording all our conversations, and that she'd use these recordings to embarrass the school and to embarrass me?

And that is what happens if you're a Royal Spare. It's very difficult to know who you can trust.

You can trust your close family – or at least most of them. The ones you can't trust, you quickly tumble to. You can trust very long-standing friends – the troupers who can be trusted to haul you out of the shit. You

68

could probably trust the Archbishop of Canterbury.

But as for the rest of the world... you just don't know.

Most people are honest and straightforward. You can trust them.

And if you were an everyday civilian, it wouldn't make much odds if you couldn't trust them – because they're never going to be in a position to turn you over.

But being a Royal Spare... that's different.

Wherever you go in the world, you will always have people sucking up to you, being nice to you. You will go years on end without ever hearing the word 'No'.

But you don't ever know why these people are being nice to you. Some are being nice because they've got a touch of Red Carpet Fever. These people just like hanging around the Royals.

Others are being nice because they want to sleep with you and perhaps even become a Royal themselves.

I don't know – there are hundreds of reasons why people want to suck up to the Royals. They're parasites but they're relatively harmless. You better get used to them.

And then there are the sharks.

Of course Heirs get their fair share of sharks and parasites. Maybe Heirs don't get up to the same amount of naughtiness that we Spares do. They are brought up to be square and respectable and straight. Spares don't have to be like that – which means we are much more of a magnet for sharks.

There are sharks everywhere. You are going to have to learn to spot them and you are going to have to learn to deal with them. The sharks are the people

69

who are looking to stiff you and to make money out of you – and the most common way this is done is to befriend you, to take some tasty video footage of you, and then to sell it.

There are other ways – as I learned from my art teacher.

So watch out for the sharks. They're always going to be there. You've got to learn to trust your instincts. The sharks can be very, very deceptive. They can be charming and funny – and the next moment they've turned you over.

So, my advice, little one, is to cultivate your intuition. Learn to trust it. If somebody is giving off a bad vibe, then there's probably a reason. You don't need to analyse that reason – just go with your gut.

You're going to be meeting a lot of people in your life. And, really, you only want to be trusting those people who you know you can trust. If you're not sure you can trust them... then don't trust them. Don't let them get their phones out, or they will stitch you up like a kipper.

Some day, some far-off day, some random stranger will come along and will promise you the moon. They will spell out your wildest fantasy and they will promise to make it flesh.

Well it might be true.

But more likely it isn't – more likely it's going to be a shark, swimming around, scenting blood, trying to stitch you up just like your great-aunt Sophie was stitched up by the Fake Sheik.

Let's face it: a guy comes along promising you the moon. He's promising you everything you ever wanted.

70

Chances of him being genuine – and of genuinely delivering? Pretty slim.

Chances of him being just another shark? I'd say it was odds-on.

One of the perks of being a Spare is that the whole world wants to be your friend. And that rather means you've got to learn to be selective.

Stretching through Windsor Great Park is an avenue of trees and a long thin ribbon of tarmac. At one end is Windsor Castle and at the other is a little hillock with a statue, the Copper Cow. (It's actually the Copper Horse with a King on top, but at school we called it the Copper Cow. That's Eton for you.) The road that connects the castle with the Copper Cow is called the Long Walk and it's nearly three miles long – though the first time I was made to walk it, when I was aged seven, it seemed to go on for ever. I walked and walked and walked with my father, and after three hours, we still weren't any closer.

Later on, I tried it on a bike. I was alone – up on the hill with the Copper Cow and it was just dusk, the sky streaked with fingers of orange and magenta.

And off I went – pedalling like an absolute maniac, the wind whipping at my face, tears streaking my cheeks. This glorious sense of freedom. I know that a lot of people experience this every single day of their lives, but it's not so common when you're an HRH.

Within a few years, I had graduated to motorbikes. Much more speed and much more power. And, much more seductive. You have complete anonymity. With my helmet on, I am just another biker – just another guy out on the road.

When I'm out on my bike, I'm usually accompanied by one of my security guards. But a few years back, I managed to lose him – and so there I was, careening through London on my Ducati.

I stopped at some traffic lights. There was a guy next to me on a big old BMW. I thought I'd show him who was boss and when the lights changed I roared off – left him in my dust.

A hundred yards later, I have to stop at the next set of lights, and as they change to green, the man on the BMW effortlessly cruises past. And as he does so, he lets me know what he thinks of me by giving a quick flick of his hand – the universal gesture for a wanker.

A lot of people would have been outraged. He was calling me a wanker! To my face!

But I was thrilled! In your life as a Spare, you'll get a lot of compliments. You'll get a lot of people licking your boots. This was the first time I'd ever been given the wanker-hand.

It was a very small taste of what it is to lead a normal life.

And my tip is – just as soon as you are able, learn to ride a motorbike. There is nothing else on earth that offers you this wonderful anonymity. Just flick down your helmet visor and in one second you are a nobody. Car-drivers will cut you up on the road. You'll get abused. You may even get the finger. But, for the first time, you will be treated just like a normal human being. It's bloody brilliant.

On Jobs

I'm not absolutely sure this was the worst decision my Uncle Edward ever made – but it was certainly in the top three.

Edward was trying to get into the Marines, and he was having a hard time of it. The Marines like to beast all of their new boys, and I guess that they really, really wanted to beast Edward because he was a Prince and because, I suppose, he was more namby-pamby than roughy-toughy. If he'd thought about it beforehand, he could probably have worked that out. The Marines are... the Marines! They're a tough bunch. It's not the easiest outfit to join. And if you were a Prince, then I think they'd make it even harder. Raise that bar just a little bit higher. Beast you just that little bit more – just to see if you've got what it takes.

He should have gone for something cosy. Like the Household Regiment. One of those ones where you've got a cushy billet in London, lots of parties, not much fighting.

Anyway, Edward had set his heart on the Marines – perhaps just to please my grandad, heart of gold but a bit of a curmudgeon – and so he joined the Marines.

And then quit the Marines.

And then tried to get into showbiz by working for Lord Lloyd-Webber.

And tried to get into TV production, even sending a crew up to St Andrews to monster your daddy Prince Billy.

None of it really worked out.

So now he lives in a big old house, Victorian,

hideous, and he spends his days opening fetes, launching ships, planting trees, being the face of Her Majesty, and doing all that unbelievably boring Royal shite that drives me just crazy.

And he'll be doing it till the day he dies.

Same with my Uncle Andrew, who also knows quite a bit about being the Spare Heir.

Used to fly helicopters for the navy. Saw action during the Falklands War. Loved it.

And then gave it all up to become 'Britain's special representative for shopping', swanning round the world to fly the Union Jack and bang the drum for all things British.

Ho-hum.

Well it's a life – of sorts.

But it also happens to be:

Boring.
Meaningless.
Drivel.

This is the truth of it.

If you are a human being, then you need a job. If you are the Spare, then you will definitely need a job – though preferably in the forces. Or, if it takes your fancy, doing what Big Billy does and flying helicopters for Search and Rescue.

Of course if you're a Royal Spare, you might want to try your hand at some other things. Maybe you'll want to be a teacher. Or a musician. Or an actor. Or a big-swinging trader on Wall Street. Or a musical impresario. (Or even a TV documentary-maker.)

Not that you can't do these things.

But it's not easy.

74

The services on the other hand... they're very easy. They are geared up for the Royals. Plus you don't permanently have the Press on your case about either a) cashing in your connections b) being a sponging Royal low-life.

The reason it's not easy holding down a normal every-day job is quite simply because you're a Royal Highness. You have the initials HRH in front of your name.

No big deal.

And yet to a lot of people it's a massive deal.

And those three little letters mean that it takes an absolute age to cut through the Royal ice. There are going to be a lot of people out there who will be in awe of you just because you're Royal. (Along with all those other sharks and parasites and flunkies. I guess what I'm saying is that there are not many people out there who are authentic and genuine. Well there may be a few. But if you're an HRH, it's not easy to find them.)

And so, ineluctably, you end up in the services, just as all the Royal Spares have done over the centuries.

The services are great – for a number of reasons. Adventure. A very defined career structure. People who boss you about. People to be bossed about.

Above all, you eventually start to deal with people who like you for who you are. Who – in time – couldn't care less whether you're an HRH. All they're really concerned about is whether you can do your job. If you're perky with it, then so much the better.

You may even find that – unbelievably – you enjoy your work! It can happen!

Me? I love helicopters! I love flying helicopters. And – well, no swanks but – I'm pretty good at flying helicopters! Who ever would have thought it with my B-grade and D-grade A-levels?

Let me tell you about the alternative to having a career.

Every morning, for the rest of your life, you will wake up, and you will have breakfast prepared for you, and then you will put on some nice clothes and you will be chauffeured to some new place. It may be a long journey, it may be a short journey.

You will arrive at your destination and there you will meet a lot of people who are very well dressed and very smiley – and who, for the most part, will be very, very nervous of you. That's part of the turf when you're an HRH.

They will bow or curtsey, some of them may stutter, and then, for the rest of your visit, you will have to make small talk. Not big talk. Not anything of any moment. Not anything that's of any interest whatsoever. You have to talk small.

You will then open the building. Unveil the plaque. Plant the tree. Launch the boat. Make the speech. Fly the flag. Make the cake. Eat the lunch. God knows what you're going to have to do, but what I can tell you is that in a very short time you realise that it is all so utterly meaningless. It is pointless. To these people, you are as real as Santa Claus or Mary Poppins. You're this mythical person who's arrived on time to launch the launch and talk small – and heaven forbid that you should start making jokes, because then you're sometimes going to put your foot in it, just as grandad does.

But is it any wonder that my grandad (that's your great-grandad) occasionally puts his foot in it? Talking small is very dull indeed, and so sometimes the old boy likes to pep things up. He makes a little quip, and it might be in dubious taste, but if it were anyone else it would all be forgotten – though since it happens to have come out of the mouth of a Prince, then the next day it's all over the front pages.

I ain't whining.

I'm telling you how it is.

And that is: you need a job. And you keep onto that job for as long as you can. Why is your daddy back flying helicopters for Search and Rescue?

It's because any job – any job at all – is better than this living, withering death of having to small talk with awe-struck strangers.

My uncle Eddie gave up life with the Marines because he thought it was tough. Compared to the Marines, small-talking is off the Richter Scale of toughness.

TOP PRINCE HARRY
JOKES: #6
Just saw on the news that
Harry is learning how to fly a
helicopter.
He's already got a flying
broomstick —
what more does he want?

☆ UNCLE ANDY'S IMPOSSIBLE DREAM

Your Great-Uncle Andy nearly found his dream career. He nearly discovered his grand strategy.

He was one of the nearly guys.

Close but no cigar.

He never quite had the guts to follow it through.

Instead, Andy has spent his days going up and down, up and down, on the Royal carousel, and the music plays, and the horses go round and the people wave, and I may not know much but what I do know is that long, long after you are dead, that Royal carousel will still be going round, and the music will still be playing and the people will still be waving and the horses will still be going up and down.

Know what Andy likes doing?

Andy likes playing golf.

He did his best to introduce me and Billy to golf, but we never took to it. (Billy's been completely phobic about the game ever since another kid thwacked him on the head with a golf club.)

Anyway – it's not really for me, but as for your Great-Uncle Andy, he is probably happiest when he is out on the golf course hitting white balls into small holes.

So… since golf was his passion, then he should have found some way to incorporate it into his life.

What about… getting on side with a few of the world's best golfers?

Creating your own golf course. Complete with hotel.

You could even put the word 'Royal' into the title.

Invite the world's top golfers to come play there. (And if you're the Royal Spare, they will come.)

And finally... setting up some form of kiddy scholarship to introduce under-privileged children to the joys of hitting golf balls.

If Uncle Andy had done that, then every single day of the week he could have got to play golf with the world's greatest players. He could have had his own perch right by the club-house bar. Could have had his own table, his own suite of rooms – his own everything. And the British Press would have been praising him to the sky for the wonderful job he'd done in introducing golf to the masses.

But as it is, all Andy ever really amounted to was being a bit of a Royal hanger-on.

Find your passion. ☆
Go for it.

If it all goes to pot, here are my top ten small talk lines
(as mostly patented by Her Majesty The Queen):

1

'That looks like a very fine medal/award/insignia/ gong/garter that you're wearing. How the devil did you earn it?'

2

'I'll bet there's an interesting story behind that amazing tie/ear-ring/necklace/brooch/tongue-stud.'

3

'Who would have thought that Prince Albert's greatest contribution to the English language was to be immortalised by a ring through your willy?'

4

'No I'm not Prince Harry – I'm his double. Fancy a snog?'

5

'Did you know the Queen dunks her biscuits – otherwise they hurt her dentures?'

6

'I have frequently told Prince Billy to wear a wig – but he just won't listen.'

7

'It sure was expensive learning to fly an Apache – but when it comes to Xbox games, I'm the King.'

8

'What's it like being a Spare? Not great – but it is a whole lot better than not even being an HRH.'

9

'What winks and shags like a tiger?'
'I don't know.'
(Wink)
(This is a personal fave, though probably not one for sharing.)

'You are incredibly beautiful and I am a Royal. Fancy a quickie?'

(This line only works about one in ten, but it can get you out of a hole if you're really stuck for something to say.)

TACTICS, STRATEGY, GRAND STRATEGY

The toughest few months I ever had were at Staff College when I was trying to cram my head with millions of pages of military academia.

I could fly helicopters just fine.

But that wasn't going to be worth a damn if I couldn't pass the exams.

Ball-breakingly tough!

As a rule, us Royals are not famous for our brains. We scrape rather than fly through our exams.

One of our teachers was this bristling Colonel, Colonel Lawson Douglas, very peppery, full handlebar moustache.

He was telling us about tactics.

And strategy.

And grand strategy.

What the hell is grand strategy?

And this is what that mad old Colonel used to scream at us:

'Tactics win you battles! Strategy wins you wars! Grand strategy is what you're planning to do after the war is won! It's your long, long-term goal.'

And what's sauce for the generals is also sauce for the Royals.

Spares need grand strategy – otherwise they'll go clean off their rockers for boredom.

If you don't have a plan, then your life is spent in constant fire-fighting. You lurch from one crisis to the next. Hard work and dispiriting with it.

Grand strategy on the other hand... you've got a purpose! You've got a goal – an impossible dream. It doesn't matter that it's impossible.

You're on a journey. And the destination, should you ever get there, will probably be a load of horse dung.

But life is sweeter when you're on a journey.

☆ **Just don't forget to stop and smell the flowers.**

ROYAL DUTIES

Another hospital trip and another round of Royal duties, and though this time it's wounded soldiers, I'm not exactly looking forward to it.

What can I do? What can anyone do for these guys?

I'm just a Prince mouthing platitudes. I sit with these severely wounded guys and listen to their stories, and then I move on and they're still stuck there with no legs and only half an arm, and that's how it's going to be for them for the rest of their lives.

I was at Selly Oak, the military hospital in Birmingham that deals with the most critical injuries. The guys there are in a very bad way, and yet the place is full of humour and compassion.

I spoke to one man. He was laughing right to the end. A few hours after I'd gone, the doctors gave him a mobile phone so that he could say goodbye to his wife.

If you ever need a pick-me-up, get yourself to somewhere like Selly Oak. These limbless men and women are in a living hell. And yet for them it's not a hell, a lot of them are genuinely enjoying themselves. They're making the most of what they've got.

It helps to put things into perspective.

Of course, when you're at Selly Oak, it feels like there's nothing at all that you can do for these guys.

But actually there is.

A few days later, Billy and I were sent a few Help For Heroes wristbands. Little rubbery wristbands. We'd never seen anything like them before. We didn't think much of it, but anyway, since they thought it might help, we put the wristbands on.

And... what do you know...

Suddenly these bits of rubber had become must-have accessories.

They were selling by the million. Six months later, the wristbands had helped raise £4 million for Help For Heroes.

And it all started when an Heir and a Spare decided, just for the hell of it, to wear a wristband.

Being an icon does occasionally have its advantages.

The Princes in the Golden Cage ☆

The Sultans in the Ottoman Empire had a crazy way of dealing with their Heirs and their Spares. Weird – but at the time, it made a lot of sense.

I have been to Topkapi Sarayi, which is the Ottoman Palace in Istanbul.

You can smell the madness.

Let me tell you the story.

Because no matter how bad things get for you, just remember what happened to the Princes in the Golden Cage.
☆

When the Ottoman Sultan died, he was not necessarily succeeded by his eldest son.

The Sultan had a number of wives and perhaps a score of sons – so why would he want to limit himself to just the eldest Heir?

Instead of going to the eldest son, the Sultan's title went to the most 'capable' son. The one who would be best able to expand the empire, keep the frontiers secure, that sort of thing. No Spares in the Ottoman Empire – every single one of the Sultan's legitimate sons was a runner and rider in the Great Ottoman Succession Handicap.

What in fact tended to happen was that the top job went to the biggest bastard.

The first thing that bastard would do when he came to the throne was have all his brothers executed. It became enshrined in law, because the very last thing that the Ottomans wanted was a civil war.

'The Killing of the Spares' – as they might have called it – reached its peak in 1595 when Mehmed III came to the throne. He had all nineteen of his brothers executed on the same night. The Palace eunuchs strangled the lot of them, one by one, with a bow string.

Just for good measure, Mehmed III then had all his sisters executed – and then his mother!

One crazy cat!

Eight years later, when Mehmed III died, his son Ahmed I came to the Ottoman throne.

And Ahmed dreamt up this amazing new way to deal with the Spares.

He didn't want to murder his brothers.

But he couldn't let them go either – because otherwise they'd kill him.

So instead, Ahmed devised this lifestyle that came to be known as 'Cage Life'.

For over 300 years, all the Heirs and Spares were kept in these luxurious suites of rooms in the Palace harem. These rooms were known as the cages. The Heirs and Spares could have all the food they wanted, all the drink and drugs – and as for women, they were kept well supplied with the greatest beauties of the Ottoman Empire.

The only problem being that there were only two ways out of the cages: you either had to become the next Sultan, or you had to die.

Many of the Princes went clean round the bend.

When Cage Life ended just over a hundred years ago, it was thought to be barbaric.

But in fact, Cage Life is all around us now.

Cage life is everywhere. The only difference being that these days we make our own cages.

The Royal family has now developed its own peculiar version of Cage Life. We attend our Royal duties. We get to lead this wonderfully pampered life. But it takes considerable force of will to prevent it from becoming your very own Golden Cage.

ENJOY TIME WITH THE KIDS

Even though I had a full-time job with the army, I still did the odd bit of ribbon-snipping. Normally I leave that sort of garbage to Uncles Eddie or Andy, but just to show willing, I would sometimes go off and snip a ribbon myself.

I liked going to hospitals, orphanages, schools – anywhere, really, which might have young children with no idea who I am.

I was on a night visit to Great Ormond Street hospital. Just popped my head in and was being shown around one of the wards.

One of the girls was not at all well. I'd just got to her bedside when she turned and threw up all over me. It was a projectile vomit, which spattered the whole of my chest.

There was this stunned silence – and then the other kids started screaming with laughter. I must have been one hell of a sight, my neatly ironed blue shirt now covered in patches of red spaghetti Bolognese.

Within a few seconds, I had started laughing too.

The nurse was laughing, and even the little girl who'd been sick was laughing. The whole ward was this warm wall of laughter.

You'd never get that with adults. Adults would be mortified at seeing a Royal covered in kiddy-sick.

So that's why I love being with kids. Kids who will scream at me, crawl all over me, laugh with me – laugh at me. Kids will treat me just like any other human being.

By the time they're about seven, it's usually too late. They'll have been told that I'm a real 'Prince', and the moment that I walk into the room, their eyes just pop out of their heads and they can't say a single word.

But so long as the younger kids haven't been primed by their parents, then they're just brilliant. They are normal and natural and authentic. There's not a fake bone in their bodies.

Funny isn't it how we always hunger after the one thing we can never have. I know there are many people who would give anything to lead this life of idle luxury.

But for us Royal Spares, one of the things we long for is genuine interaction with another human being.

And you'll get this most with young children. Children in Britain, or children abroad, who couldn't give a damn about your title.

These are the people I love to mix with.

Children are the best way yet of keeping your feet on the ground.

Mix with them. As much as you can.

☆ PLAY TO YOUR
☆ STRENGTHS

At school, there were a lot of things that I wasn't much good at.

Classes? Formal academic classes in school?

Not really my thing, I'm afraid.

Whatever the subject, I was always and invariably with the dockers in the bottom class. Didn't matter whether it was the sciences or the arts, I was always hopeless. Out of 250 boys, I was – literally – the thickest boy in the entire year.

However, there were some things that I was quite good at.

I wasn't bad at sport. (Not as good as Big Bruv Billy, but he was always much more keen. He'd put in the hours, whereas I always saw sport as being a pleasant interlude from attending lessons.)

And there was one other thing that I was good at.

Rather frowned on at the time. It was something 'saddos' used to do. Well I was that saddo – and I became quite good at it.

I'm talking computer games.

I think it would be fair to say that during my time at Eton, I gave those poor little computer games a very sound thrashing. Homework? Forget it! I had better things to do like pulverising onscreen tanks and blasting bad guys.

I must have been spending about five hours a day playing them. I was spending so long at these games, that the next day I often looked pale, pasty-faced, hollow-eyed. (Though there may admittedly have been other reasons for that.)

By the time I left Eton, I was one hell of a hot-shot at computer games. Best in the school. If there'd been an opportunity available, I reckon I could have been a computer game scholar; could have become a Professor of Computer Games. Quick reactions – know what I mean?

It did all help turn me into a pretty useful helicopter pilot. A helicopter is just a vast computer game, with lots of buttons to press. The more lightning-quick your reactions, the better you'll be.

Who ever would have thought it? A computer games wizard turns into a top gun.

In life you will have weaknesses, you will have strengths. You want to play to your strengths.

It is important to know what your weaknesses are. In my case, this pretty much involved anything at all to do with lessons, reading or study.

Fine! These are my weaknesses. I was never going to force it. I did the minimum to get by.

But I did have a strength – and that was, of course, computer games. Computer games may not be everyone's cup of tea, but I liked them.

And, after a while, I started playing to my strength. And who could have guessed how well it's all turned out. Quite unwittingly, computer games have provided me with the most perfect career possible. And what's more… I love it!

Stick that to all those grunting drones with their A-grade A-levels, and their fancy Honours Degrees!

INVICTUS

I've played a fair number of brutal games. Punchy games of rugby and football; plenty of knocks on the polo field.

There are many hungry people out there who are only too happy to take a chunk out of a member of the Royal Family. These guys are out to win and they positively relish the prospect of trampling over a young prince.

Gouging. Biting. Knees to the groin. ☆

I've seen a lot of unpleasantness in sport.

But nothing - nothing at all - will ever come to touching the sheer thuggishness of playing with paraplegics.

I have played many games with disabled people. Baseball, handball, netball, you name it, I have been strapped into that wheelchair, I have crawled all over the ground, I have got stuck in.

And what I know is that these guys really, really want to win. The women are even worse! It's their life mission not just to win, but to grind you into dust beneath their wheels.

This is a very, very good thing.

It empowers the handicapped and the disabled. It gives them great joy and a great sense of purpose.

Took me a few years to work out – but as soon as I had worked it out, I knew that I wanted to do something about it. I wanted to harness that competitive spirit.

And – unlike almost everyone else on earth – I could do something about it.

That's because even though I'm a Spare, I'm a Prince. And that means that powerful people listen to me.

It is a wonderful gift. **Spares can do things which other people cannot.** We can bend the ears of the rich and the great and the beautiful.

In my case, I used that power to create the Invictus Games.

I'm very proud of these games. They are a small thing, but they are my own.

A word of warning though.

Spares can get people to listen, but it is a power that must be used judiciously. Frugally. And with discretion.

Come up with too many fliers, too many off-the-wall ideas and people will stop listening.

Just take a look at Prince Eddie after he came up with the crazy 'It's A Royal Knockout!' madness!

I don't think Eddie has ever really recovered.

PICK YOUR BATTLES

☆ ☆

Here's a little factoid that I gleaned at Staff College. Forgotten most of that bilge, but for some reason this one stuck with me.

When he was out riding, the Duke of Wellington loved to survey the countryside for potential battle sites.

He'd come across the fields at Waterloo a full year before he fought the actual battle.

Then he plans, he manoeuvres, he strategises, and then eventually he's got Napoleon in the right position.

And when – and only when – Napoleon is in

exactly the right position does Wellington decide to have a battle.

He's picked his battle!

Meaning? (I had a crazy English teacher at Eton, Nick Welsh. Hi Nick! Nick used to love that word. You'd spout some claptrap that you'd memorised from a textbook, and then he'd just stand there swaying in front of your desk shouting, 'Meaning? Meaning? What does that actually mean? What is its meaning?')

Anyway – meaning that as an HRH you want to pick your battles very, very carefully indeed.

And, generally, you do not want to engage.

Don't have a row. Don't blow your top!

Remember – you're a Royal! You're waited on hand and foot. You've got a whole army of flunkies attending to your every whim. So most of the time it's a pretty bad idea to lose your rag. For instance, if there's been a cock-up and you're tired and hungry. Just soak it up. That's what you have to do when you're a Royal.

But the thing is, you mustn't soak it up all the time. Sometimes, though not very often, you've got to blow your top. Just to show you're not a pushover.

At some stage you are going to have to have a battle – just to show that you're not a total wet blanket. No offence, Uncle Eddie.

This is how it was with me.

I'd been in the army for a few years, was an okay troop commander, just minding my own business. Then one of the gunners in my section told me that he was being bullied. He was twenty-one and he was one of the first openly gay men in the army. Six sergeants had threatened to 'batter' him for spreading false rumours.

The ideal battleground.

A great matter of principle.

Sticking up for one of the guys.

Just.

About.

Perfect.

So, as I said, when you're a Royal you have to spend a lot of time soaking things up. Lots of waiting around: soak it up. Lots of meaningless chit-chat: soak it up. Lots of shaking hands: soak it up.

You soak it up and you soak it up until one day you are able to vent, and when that day comes – when you finally decide to fight that battle – then, in comparison, Krakatoa is just going to be a mere fart in a hurricane.

I found those six sergeants. Let's just say that I don't think they'd ever been spoken to like that before by an officer.

Let alone a Royal.

I reamed them each a new arsehole.

Worked like a charm.

Pick your battles.

And when you pick 'em, go in with full force.

Once you're in, you better damn well make sure you win!

Spam. I bet you hate spam. Clogging up your inbox. All those crappy messages, all of them just eating into your playtime.

I've got a confession.

I LOVE Spam.

Adore it.

Though perhaps you may not have tried this particular kind of Spam.

I'm not talking about all that internet shite. Can't be doing with that.

I'm talking about the meaty Spam. The tinned Spam. The pink stuff that's a bit like corned beef.

Well – when the timing's right, this Spam is the very food of the Gods.

We'd been out on exercise in the tanks for over five days, and as usual the tank had broken down. (That's the weird thing about tanks. You think they're unstoppable. Well this is what I know: absolutely anything can stop them. A small piece of grit in the air filter, a loose wheel bearing, you bloody name it. You spend more time waiting for your tank to be repaired than you ever do actually driving the thing.)

My gay trooper friend rummaged about in his rucksack and produced some oil and a tin of Spam.

I was pretty dubious. 'What's this shite?'

'Just wait until you've tried it.'

He sliced up the Spam, fried it. Smothered it in enough Tabasco sauce to blow your head off.

It was delicious. Though mind you, it did probably help that we'd only been on army rations for the previous five days.

These days, I never leave home without a tin of Spam at the bottom of the bag. Spam, eh? Who knew? Yet another little thing that keeps me sane.

The Hot and the Cold

Out in Afghanistan, the heat sometimes reached fifty degrees.

That is cosy.

Let me tell about fifty degree heat. It is drinking eleven litres of water – and never once needing to pee. You are sweating out the water just as fast as you pour it in. The sweat leaves tide-lines of white scum on your face and on your neck.

I remember the heat, the barren ochre landscape, feeling so drained that I couldn't even flap at the flies as they crawled over my nose.

A year later, I was in the Arctic, lugging a sledge up to the North Pole for Help For Heroes.

A little different from Afghanistan.

Not fifty degrees, but MINUS fifty! That's a 100 – degree temperature drop – the difference between boiling water and ice.

On top of that, being battered by these constant 110-mph gales.

We were having to eat over 6,000 calories a day, mainly chocolate. And we still lost weight.

Surprised some entrepreneur hasn't already latched onto that one: The Arctic Diet – eat as much as you like and still get thin!

Two extremes, then. Equally life-enhancing.

Having experienced both, here's my tip:

Take the extreme heat over the extreme cold. Any day of the week.

The Arctic is just gruelling.
Humans are not meant to be there.

Then again – who the hell says you have to go for either one extreme or the other?

I like going on these charity challenges because it gets me out of the Royal rut. You don't tend to find so many of these deranged 'Harry Hunters' out in the Arctic.

However – it is more than likely that the Arctic – or Afghanistan – may not do it for you.

But you're still going to have to find a place where, for once, you can be yourself rather than being an HRH.

Problem is, the sort of places where you can just be yourself tend to be rather inhospitable. Very hot, or very cold, or very wet or very jungly.

If a place is pleasant, temperate and conveniently close to civilisation, then within a few hours you will find yourself surrounded by Royal junkies who want to take a bloody selfie with you.

It's a bit of a toss-up. But generally I'd plump for the extremes.

The Germans have a phrase for it: *Nicht immer, aber immer öfter.*

Not always, but often.

RED CARPET FEVER

If you are a courtier who has moved for too long in Royal circles, then you develop this very strange disease, which is known as Red Carpet Fever.

You start to believe all the hype. You start to think that the Royals are just that little bit special.

You are not paid very much. But you bask in the reflected glory that comes with being a Royal flunkie.

You begin to hanker after the little baubles that Her Majesty occasionally sees fit to dole out to her underlings. Medals, gongs, titles, everything from the Royal Victoria something-or-other all the way up to a knighthood. Some of 'em even get so far up the greasy pole they land themselves a peerage! (Much good it does them.)

These are people that have been swallowed up into the black hole that is the monarchy. Give them enough time and they'd even start to believe in the Divine Right of Kings.

It is all total flummery.

Tosh.

Once someone's got Red Carpet Fever, then they generally cease to be a human being. Suddenly it's all bowing and scraping and grovelling at your every word.

My dad sees a whole load of cases of Rampant Red Carpet Fever. Prince Billy does too.

I see it quite often. It's all rather dispiriting.

Red Carpet Fever can only really be cured by a prolonged holiday away from the Royal family and its Palaces.

But if you've had a good dose of Red Carpet Fever, then it's usually terminal.

☆ On Make-Up

One day, you will have one of the most famous faces in not just the UK but the whole world.

You will not be able to step out of your front door without instantly being recognised and then hosed down by umpteen mobile phones.

Sometimes you will just long to be a bland, normal human being – someone who can just step onto the pavement without a single person noticing you.

As I've mentioned, you can get round this by getting out on your motorbike. We love those full-face helmets!

Or, as Prince Billy and I once did a few years ago, you can hire a professional make-up artist.

Over the years, we had tried wigs and hats, but it never seemed to make any difference, someone always spotted us.

So this time round, a make-up artist spent a couple of hours making us completely unrecognisable. I'd never had a session like it. Just sitting there, utterly relaxed, as Prince Harry was erased and in his place appeared just this ordinary-looking guy, different nose, different skin-colour. With the black wig, I looked slightly Hispanic.

Prince Billy's transformation was equally complete. The make-up artist had turned him into a blonde; he looked like a Swede.

We put on fresh clothes that we'd bought online from Next.

And then out we skulked through the tradesman's entrance at Clarence House. It wasn't quite as we'd have liked it, as our security man Gary had to tag along too – but Gary was also dressed down in jeans and a bomber jacket. He kept a discreet distance.

We mooched up Pall Mall and into a pub off Oxford Street. Packed with tourists! We were slumming it! Nobody had a clue. Not much for anyone else – but for a couple of young Princes, it was wonderful.

I edged over to the bar and waved for a drink. And was promptly ignored by the barman who instead served a pretty brunette standing next to me. Not an experience I'd ever had before.

I started to chat to the pretty brunette – said something like, 'Do you always get served so promptly?'

And guess what happens? She utterly blanks me! She rolls her eyes, takes her bottle of white wine and then goes to join her three friends.

Blanked by a woman! Another new experience!

I got in a couple of pints and then, beautiful moment, Billy and I just sat down on a couple of bar stools and we… blended right in! Nobody knew us from Adam! I even tried chatting up the beautiful brunette again and guess what happened? She blanked me! Again!

For the first time in our lives we were doing just exactly what everyone else takes for granted – having a quiet drink with a mate without being pestered by some total tool who wants your photo and/or autograph.

Then and there, we decide to make a night of it. We were going to go on an old-fashioned pub crawl, anonymously cruising through central London.

We mooched up Oxford Street, eventually wound

up at Holborn and then Fleet Street, and then just for the bloody hell of it, we went into El Vino's. El Vino's, in case you don't know, is that Seventh Circle of Hell where the scum-sucking hacks go to drink.

Talk about putting your head in the lion's mouth! Seemed like a good idea at the time.

Going into El Vino's was not an error in itself.

But we did make two mistakes.

Firstly: we may have transformed our looks, but we certainly had not transformed our voices. Billy, in particular, has quite a recognisable voice. To be blunt, he sounds like a toff.

When we'd first started out drinking, we'd kept our voices quite low, but by the time we were on our sixth pint, Billy was giving it full volume.

Not dangerous in itself. But fairly dangerous in a place like El Vino's.

The second mistake was our copper, Gary. Gary who'd just spent the whole evening soberly nursing his juices as Billy and I got more and more sloshed.

Gary would generally go into the pubs ahead of us, case the joint and then order a juice for himself – can't drink on duty – before taking a quiet table in the corner.

When we went into El Vino's, we just followed Gary straight in – might even have been actually talking to him.

And then Gary peels off to buy his juice.

The problem being that while Billy and I may have been completely unrecognisable, Gary most certainly wasn't. In Fleet Street circles, he was quite well known. He was the Royal cop who looked after Prince William and Prince Harry.

Add to that our odd behaviour.

And then the clincher: every time Billy opened his mouth, out came this unmistakable Hooray drawl.

They'd rumbled us in about three minutes flat.

A guy in a sharp blue suit sidles over to our table and innocuously starts a conversation, 'Phew – what a night!' he says with a grin.

And being just the regular guys we are, we get into a sort of conversation. But something is not right.

At least I'll say one thing for the army. You learn to trust your instincts. You may not know quite why a situation is wrong – but if that sixth sense goes off, then get the hell out.

We got the hell out.

They'd still got a few pictures – chasing out after us onto the street.

So here's my advice:

You need a Royal make-up artist so that, just as often as you feel like it, you can become a regular human being.

But. You've got to change your voice.

Not elocution lessons – but delocution lessons.

Make sure that you don't use your regular security man.

Oh, and one thing more. When you're out on the lash, don't pop into El Vino's or any other pub that is frequented by journalists. Just as we

Army boys develop a sixth sense for danger, so hacks have acquired very acute antennae for ☆ Royalty.

THE DOUBLE

Ten years back, while I was on my gap year before going to Sandhurst, I had a stint playing polo in Argentina. The world's best polo players all come from Argentina; they are practically born in the saddle and, within fifteen years, they are world class.

I was only just out of Eton and I was relatively well behaved. No clubbing for little Harry, and instead I spent my time at the El Remanso polo farm.

Not that you'd have known it though from the British papers, which were awash with stories of my drunken excesses. Stories of me sneaking out of the ranch to go clubbing. Stories of me copping off with some local girl. There was even some crazy tale that there'd been a plot to kidnap me.

All of it total bollocks – in the usual tabloid way of things.

For once, I hadn't set a foot wrong.

For once, Prince Ginger had not been out partying. Crazy but true.

No – rather bizarrely it turned out that I had a double, and this guy had been trading off my looks to guzzle free booze in the local club and score with the local talent.

Good for him! I mean it can't have been easy for this guy if he had ginger hair and looked just like me. But seeing that I'd been staying in the vicinity he

102

had at last come into his own.

In World War II, General Montgomery had a double. This double was sent first-class all over the world, thereby duping the Nazis.

And what I know is that every Royal also ought to have a double.

The double probably wouldn't be able to pass muster for your official Royal duties.

But where the doubles could come into their own is when you're on holiday.

There you are, say, on some charming estate in Tuscany, and meanwhile the paparazzi are all waiting outside, and doubtless climbing up the trees so that they can take long-range pictures of you with their Big Tom lenses.

And they're welcome to all the shots they can get of you larking around at your Tuscan mansion house – because it's not in fact you, it's your double, who's being paid a couple of grand to sit by the pool for a fortnight and sip lager.

The double takes the hacks off the scent.

You, meanwhile, are off on a genuine holiday without a single paparazzo to be seen. And when some bovine holiday-maker comes up to you in the café and says, 'Do you know you look just like Prince Harry?', you smoothly reply, 'Yeah, worst luck.' And then you give them a wry smile and add: 'It doesn't help that James Hewitt was seeing Mum for a while…'

So, find yourself a double. ☆
Make use of them.

Nothing will make your day quite so much as selling a dummy to the paparazzi.

THE YIN AND YANG OF ROYALTY ☆

This is perhaps going to sound a little odd coming from an army uncle who's as daft as a brush – but I'll have a shot.

I'm going to give you a small slice of Taoism. Yin and Yang. Black and white. Philosophy. Theology. Life. All that good stuff.

In the 6th century BC, while the Greeks were busily creating the world's first democracy, there was a Chinese sage called Lao Tzu.

Lao Tzu had been doing a lot of thinking about life, and eventually wrote the Tao Te Ching. This text was to become the bedrock of Taoism.

(Still with me? Want more tales of naughtiness? Do not worry – there's more to come.)

Here's what Lao Tzu painted in his elegant script:

'When people see some things as beautiful, other things become ugly.'

This is the fundamental core of the universe. Everything has its opposite. For every black there has to be a white.

Which very roughly translates as: for every single Royal fan out there, there will also be a person who loathes the Royals.

There are a whole load of people who love the Royals.

Therefore there must also be a whole load of people out there who hate us.

That's not just Taoism. That's life.

There's no point in complaining about being hated by large swathes of society. You can't do a thing about it.

You will never, not in a million years, be able to win round a single one of these Republican toe-rags. They hate the Royals. They hate everything we stand for.

It's part of the turf.

Being a Royal Spare, you are going to cause a lot of very intense reactions, some pleasant, some not so much.

Going to be a lot of people out there who hate you for what you are.

Forget 'em!

They're not worth bothering about. They are a part of the universe. For every fan that you have, there has to be somebody else who hates you.

Somehow, some way, you'll just have to see if you can console yourself with that other army of beauties who are so besotted by the Royals that they'll kiss the very ground you walk on.

LIGGERS

I once had a friend in the army. I was his commanding officer. Let's call him Archie.

I quite enjoyed Archie's company and we had some good banter – but there was always something about him that didn't smell quite right.

Couldn't put my finger on it for a long, long time.

And then, after I'd known Archie about a year, he asked me if I could blag him some tickets to Royal Ascot.

Obvious, really. I was the Royal Spare, Ascot had the word 'Royal' in front of it, and so therefore I must have a limitless supply of tickets.

Talk about taking the piss!

Actually, Archie did me a real favour by asking for those tickets, because that's when I knew he was a waste of space. He was a ligger.

Liggers are the toe-rags who blag their way into parties so that they can hoover up all the free booze. Liggers love sucking up to the Royals because, of course, they think you'll be a great contact who will invite them to lots of smart parties.

Liggers are the bane of an HRH's life.

They're often very smooth. Charming.

They can be intensely beautiful.

Very difficult to weed out the liggers from the real thing.

But they're complete blood-suckers. Give them the chance and they will suck you dry.

**You need very acute antennae to spot them.
Sometimes it's just the tiniest whiff.**

The sooner you start developing these antennae, the better. It's almost a gut feeling. And when you get that feeling, then go with your gut.

(And if anyone, apart from perhaps your big brother, ever asks you for tickets to Royal Ascot, they are by definition a ligger.)

THE PAPARAZZI

Most photographers are probably okay.
    Probably.   ☆

Okay – possibly.

Perhaps it's just that I've come across more than my fair share of a-holes. I'm certainly a pretty big target.

And that's fine. I can deal with photographers – even when they're sticking their lenses right in my face.

What I had a lot of difficulty in coming to terms with was the baiting. Photographers love to see if they can provoke.

They'll call you the most foul names just to see if they can get a rise.

And as for your mum – the lovely, lovely Duchess of Katiness – they regularly used to call her a bitch and a slapper and much worse. Just to get the pictures of her losing her temper. Those pictures would be worth a lot of money.

But Kate is so serene that she never rises to the bait.

I used to, though not so much these days.
So, I know this is going to be very, very difficult. But if you possibly can, you are going to have to avoid losing your temper. Particularly in public.

**The paps will try to incite you any way
they can.
You've just got to rise above it.**

(Actually – know what might work? A little pin-camera in your lapel, recording all the stuff that these monstrous photographers are yelling at you. Stick the footage up on YouTube. And then watch those buggers squirm! The biter well and truly bit!) ☆

DEALING WITH THE POLITICIANS

I must have been about thirteen the first time I met Tony Blair. It must have been soon after he'd become Prime Minister. I like to think that I soon sussed him out as a crawling grease-ball.

Very smarmy, particularly to my dad.

And his insufferable wife Cherie, with that transparently fake grin; you could just tell that she hated the Royal family and everything we stood for.

Gordon Brown when he was Prime Minister, with his bitten fingernails and the weird thing he used to do with his tongue, sort of stuffing it behind his lower lip, was equally fake – but then, like Blair, he was the Prime Minister so you can't really tell him to sling his hook.

I've met tons of these politicians, most of them oil-slicks, and these, apparently, are the people who have the power.

Which they do.

For a very short while.

Us Royals – even us Spares – have a much softer kind of power. We ask people to dinner. We bend people's ears. We rattle the swill-drum and people will give millions to our charities.

And, if we like, we hand out gongs and titles.

Ohhh – and just one more thing. The politicians are here today, gone tomorrow. For a few years, they get to live in Downing Street – and then they get bumped off to the red leather benches in the living hell of the House of Lords.

But the Royals... we roll on forever.

My granny, the Queen – she's seen sixty years' worth of Prime Ministers. She's seen them come, she's seen them go. Not much she hasn't seen, actually.

Even us Spare Heirs have quite a bit of soft power.

But you've got to have a goal. If you're not following some impossible dream, then your life becomes as vacuous as Tony Blair's.

When Blair was Prime Minister, he loved the power. Just didn't have the faintest idea what to do with it.

You really have to suck it up with the politicians.

But at least you have the consolation of knowing that within ten years, and probably less, they'll be history.

DEATH WISH

Such a crazy life that we Spares lead – though after a while it all starts to seem normal.

You spend your entire childhood surrounded by protection officers who are there for your safety. They'd take a bullet for you. They'd kill for you! The most important thing in their lives is your personal safety.

They are there to protect you from every bump and bloody scrape.

I must have been about thirteen, when Tiggy the nanny took me and Big Billy abseiling down some dam in Monmouthshire in Wales. We didn't have helmets on.

So we might have bumped our heads, or something might have dropped on us – but in all likelihood we were going to be absolutely fine. The chances of us injuring ourselves were minuscule.

That's not what you'd have thought if you'd read the newspapers. Huge row. You'd have thought that Tiggy had had us walking the tightrope over the Niagara Falls.

I spent most of my childhood being mollycoddled beyond belief.

That's probably the reason why I have such a vast appetite for danger. If an activity involves speed and the distinct possibility of doing yourself an injury, then SIGN ME UP!

I was about six years old when I first went skiing. It wasn't that I was fearless. I was absolutely bloody petrified! But that was the thrill of it – slip-sliding down these mountains of ice in Switzerland, this tight ball of terror in the pit of my stomach, and all combined with the elation of knowing that I was right on the edge of a precipice, a single slip from oblivion.

Thrilling!

Riding our scrambler bikes all around Highgrove. We were only thirteen or fourteen, but you could really pick up some speed on the dirt tracks. Just me on the bike, bouncing over the ruts and the ditches and the faster you went, the more exciting it became.

Flying an Apache helicopter while there's incoming

110

fire blazing at you from the darkness.

It's not quite a death wish. But it is the thrill of risk – whether it's risking your life or your health, or even just the risk of rank public humiliation.

It is highly addictive. You spend your days wearing this Royal straightjacket, and every so often you need to cut loose. To do the sort of things which would give your security detail a heart attack.

This is what you need to know. It IS crazy.

But you have to do these things to keep sane. If you don't do them, then you will shrink and wither like a desert cactus that's had no water, still alive, but only just.

However.

If at all possible, plump for the activities which, when they go hideously wrong, will not leave you either dead, maimed or on the front page of the papers. ☆

The Correct Route Across a Square

What on earth I am doing talking about squares and geometry? You must think I've lost the plot!

But this has nothing at all to do with maths or science.

It's about relationships.

This is the essence of dealing with anyone and everyone. From your spouse to your parents; the Heir to the bloody throne to your own children. (Now I know that's a long way off, but bear with me.)

111

All you need to remember is that age-old proverb that comes from the mists of Arabian history. They knew a few things about getting what you wanted. And the one thing – the main thing – they realised is that it's all about how you cross a square.

It is deceptively simple.

You see, there's a correct route to crossing a square and there's an incorrect route.

And, well, here it is. Here is the wisdom.

The correct route across a square is... (drum-roll, please) ☆

By three sides.

Meaning?

Meaning, meaning?

Meaning, very roughly, that if you have a goal, a desire, something you want from a parent or a spouse or a sibling or a teacher, then it's probably not best to baldly state that need.

For instance:

'Please Sir, I really want to go to McDonald's so I can stuff my face with a Big Mac and all those greasy fries.'

Might work. Probably won't work.

For instance:

'Billy, you've had two hours in the Aston Martin pedal car – can I have a go now please?'

Definitely won't work.

For instance:

'Dada, can I go to a friend's sleepover at which there will almost certainly be a hellish amount of

112

vodka and a cartload of pretty girls?'

You use your brains. You think about the problem.   ☆

Do not just announce what it is that you want. That would be like crossing a square by just one side. Too obvious. Some people – not mentioning any names, but, say, some Royal Heirs – like nothing more than pissing off Royal Spares.

If, when I was five years old, I'd gone up to Billy and asked to have a go in the toy Aston Martin, then you'd have had to have prised him out of the car with a crowbar and even then he'd still have probably slept in the thing overnight.

But what if…

What if instead of telling Billy that I wanted a go in his Aston Martin, I had worked out the three sides by which to cross this particularly awkward square.

In this case, I might, say, have developed a most profound interest in his toy tricycle. I might have started riding the tricycle round and round the garden, pushing it up the hill and then whooping with glee as I went down the hill, all the while laughing at the very top of my screechy voice at the sheer, unadulterated joy of riding Billy's bike.

Billy was probably bored witless after ten minutes in the Aston Martin, and the only thing that was still keeping him in there was the knowledge that His Royal Spareness wanted to have a go.

Once he'd realised that I couldn't care less about his rotten pedal car, and that in fact I was deliriously happy on his trike, then he'd have been out of that Aston Martin in two seconds flat.

Or another example...

Suppose at Eton I'd suddenly developed a yearning for two Big Macs and a super-sized load of fries.

The correct route across this particular square might have been to have sidled up to my housemaster, Andrew Gailey, and then said something like this: 'Please Sir, what do poor people eat?'

'We don't call them "poor", Harry m' boy, we call them disadvantaged.'

'All right Sir – what do disadvantaged people eat?'

'I'm not with you, Harry.'

'I realise, Sir, what an enormous privilege it is to be at a school like Eton, packed out with toffs 'n all that, and I was just wondering what disadvantaged people eat?'

'Well, ummm... interesting question, Harry... disadvantaged people tend to eat very similar food to you or me, except it may not be quite so healthy?'

'Is that that thing called fast food?'

'Well, ahhh, yes, I suppose that disadvantaged people do tend perhaps to eat more fast food than, ahhh, Etonians... '

'Would that be the food that is served at McDonald's?'

'Yes – quite right, Harry m' boy. And Burger King. And KFC. Kentucky Fried Chicken's not too bad, actually.'

Long pause. A pensive wistful look crosses the furrowed brow.

'But please Sir... what does fast food taste like?'

'Well, errr, I... ahhh... '

'Does it taste like chicken? Is it greasy or chewy?'

The doltish housemaster is finally struck by an arc of inspiration. 'Tell you what Harry, m' boy – why don't you find out for yourself? Here's a tenner and…'

'Will a tenner really be enough?'

'All right, all right, have a score [that's a twenty] – take along a couple of your chums and when you bring back the change, you can give me a full report.'

'Yes Sir! Indeed Sir! I will stuff my face full of Big Macs whether I like them or not, and then I'll report back on what they taste like.'

'Excellent, Harry m'boy – that's precisely the sort of get-your-hands-dirty spirit that we like to encourage at Eton…'

See? The correct route across a square is by three sides. (And if it's a very thorny problem, then sometimes the correct route across a square might be five sides, or ten sides, as you double-back on yourself and generally muddy the water.

Or that final example that I mentioned…

'Dada, can I go to a friend's sleepover at which there will almost certainly be a hellish amount of vodka and a cartload of pretty girls?'

Well this one's unusual because this is one of those times when it's probably best to go Route One. Each situation has to be weighed up on its individual merits.

And in this case I was dealing with the old man. And when it comes to the two little Princelings, his Heir and his Spare, the old man is one hell of a soft touch.

And in conclusion?

When you want something off somebody else; if you want to sweet-talk a relative; if you want to cajole somebody into doing something, then, before you do anything at all, think about it.

Treat it as a problem. Think about it some more. Does this person have a weak spot? Can you start to apply any leverage?

The more you think about a problem, the better the chances are that you'll get the result you want.

☆

THE STORY OF THE MOORHEN

☆

There's a pond at Highgrove, and on this pond there used to be a moorhen. Nothing too special about this moorhen, just your usual moorhenny kind of bird, black with a dab of yellow on his face, except that he did happen to be your grandad's favourite moorhen.

William and I had been out for a walk. We had our guns, little .410 shotguns, the sort that poachers used to use, and like any boy anywhere with a gun, we were looking to kill things. We were looking to shoot anything within range. If we'd seen a dodo strutting through the fields, then that bird would not have lasted more than three seconds.

And nor did the moorhen.

The old man's favourite moorhen.

Almost as soon as I'd seen the bird, I had the gun up to my shoulder. It was scudding across the water, about to take off, and even as I'm tracking on it, Billy is saying, 'Don't shoot that, it's Dad's favourite moorhen!'

Bang, bang and another moorhen bites the dust.

And that should have been the end of that.

I forgot all about it.

But, eventually, Billy and I are being called into Andrew Gailey's study to be grilled about a certain dead moorhen. Can you imagine? Our housemaster is quizzing us about something that's happened in the holidays. Since when did schoolmasters question boys about misdemeanours that occurred outside term time?

Gailey: 'Your father is very upset. Somebody's shot his favourite moorhen.'

Billy (altogether brighter than me): 'Moorhen? What moorhen would that be Dr Gailey? I don't know anything about any shot moorhens.'

Me (altogether thicker than Billy): 'Would that be the moorhen you told me not to shoot?'

Stupid.

Well now I know. I know **The Motto.**

This is the Eton motto. This is the army motto. This is the motto for living with the Royals, and this is the motto for life: Deny, deny, deny.

Takes a lot of practice, though. And I've had a lot of practice. Still not quite as good as Billy, but then he was always a natural.

Anyway, if you want to start making your life a whole lot easier, then you want to start denying things. Never 'fess up! Ever! Ever!

☆ JOINING UP ☆

Going to Sandhurst is, I guess, rather like getting your leg blown off by a mine.

In that you know that they're both going to be extremely painful and unpleasant experiences. You know they're going to be just awful. But even though you've been told countless times about how grim they're going to be, nothing can ever prepare you for the reality.

Not that I've had a leg blown off, but I have been to Sandhurst, and even though I knew all about it beforehand, nothing can ever really set you up for the reality.

I'd had a lot of coaching. I was as fit as a flea and really thought I knew what it was going to be like.

And it was still a shocker.

Now, my darling Charlotte, if you've got any sense, you will also end up joining one of the forces. And it doesn't much matter whether you're joining the army, the navy or the RAF, they like to make the whole experience just as unpleasant as they can. It's a good way to sort the weeds out.

You arrive with a bag of kit and an ironing board and Brasso and shoe polish and you spend the next forty-four weeks learning how to use it all. And boy do I know how to use it. I reckon I could now iron shirts for Britain – if shirt-ironing was an Olympic event, I would be a shoe-in for the podium. As for shoe-shining, give me a pair of filthy cracked boots and I could have those toe-caps gleaming like mirrors in under five minutes.

They were completely obsessed by rumples in the beds and spotless uniforms. A single out-of-place crease would have the sergeants screaming as if you'd tossed them a live grenade with the pin out. It's a wonder that Sandhurst doesn't churn out an army of obsessive compulsives who spend their lives measuring the exact correct distance between the toothbrush and the toothpaste. (There is a correct distance, but I'm damned if I know what it is.)

Tons of exercise, tons of punishment parades, tons of living outside in a hole in the ground that is steadily filling up with rainwater. And then it's up at 5am, shave and clean up, and stand by your beds and get ready for the 5.30am inspection. Over and over again. Sandhurst seems to stretch on forever.

One of the best ways to break you is – as any good torturer knows – to make sure that you are perpetually dog-tired. You get up early, you go to bed late, though not that it makes much odds when you go to bed because they're still going to wake you up in the middle of the night for whatever alarms they can concoct for you. The accommodation ain't great, but after a few days of living out in the wilderness that bunk bed becomes a fixed fantasy.

No booze in the first five weeks, no phone calls and no out-of-town jaunts allowed. No girlfriends either, come to that.

And then at the end of it all, after a good ten months, you get your commission at Sandhurst's legendary passing out ceremony. Granny, Her Majesty, turned up for mine, first time she'd come along in fifteen years – and if she's still kicking in twenty years' time, which she might well be, I don't doubt that she'll be turning up to your passing out parade too.

We had a brief word on the parade ground.

'You look very smart,' she said.

'Thank you Granny,' I replied. The starchier the occasion – and it doesn't get much starchier than the Sovereign's Parade at Sandhurst – the more I like to lower the tone by calling her Granny and calling Philip Pops. Rather odd talking to your granny while you're stiff at attention, but then again, welcome to the Royal family.

'The girls won't be able to keep their hands off you,' she says.

'No change there then, Granny.' ☆

In the evening, there was the party, the mother of all parties, the great Sandhurst Ball. After ten damn months of having to soak it up, we were finally done with the place. Billy turned up with Kate, Chelsy turned up – the whole mob were there. I have never experienced euphoria like it. It had almost been worth going through this Sandhurst hell just for the sheer pleasure of being done with it all.

At midnight, the pips on my shoulders were revealed for the first time.

I felt more proud of that, more pleased with that, than anything else I've ever done. They meant that I was a Second Lieutenant in the Household Cavalry. But, more importantly, they signified that, for ten solid months, I had managed to soak up Sandhurst's shit.

There's no thrill at all in getting something handed to you on a plate. The thrills in life come after graft and swallowing shit – and the more shit you've had to swallow, the better the feeling when you finally stop.

GETTING TO KNOW YOU

We'd been out on patrol in Afghanistan, me and my men in our four lightweight tanks, and as always happens when you're out with four tanks, one of them breaks down.

Something wrong with the engine.

We are absolutely in the middle of nowhere. It's just desert and mountains on the horizon, a landscape that won't have changed in millions of years.

We do what we have to do: we put on a brew. (Plus Spam… Can't be doing without the Spam!)

A couple of the men are tinkering around with the engine. Don't know what the hell they're doing as I'm only the troop leader – certainly not an engineer. I know one end of the tank from another, but that's about it.

I'm sipping my second cup of tea, when I hear this **'crack'** right next to my ear, as if a stone has been hurled against the side of the tank. A moment later I hear the boom of the gunshot. Another crack on the tank, and another. We're scrabbling for cover because we're under attack. Live bullets buzzing into the armour. The air is alive with the sound of bullets and ricochets.

We all dive inside the tanks.

But what are we going to do about the fourth tank that's broken down?

Leave it to the Afghans and their rifles?

Nope.

Wait till they've gone and then try and mend the thing?

Nope.

Bullets continue to pepper the tank.

'Right lads,' I said. 'Who's going to volunteer to hook up a tow. It'll only take a minute.'

No volunteers.

'I'll cite you for a medal.'

☆

I get a volunteer. Who did get his medal.

The busted tank is hitched up and we escape without further mishap.

We celebrated later with a few beers. We'd been under live fire and we'd done the business.

Going to war is probably the best method in history of bonding with another human being.

There are other ways to bond.

Alcohol is always brilliant. Alcohol breaks down many barriers.

But the ties that last a lifetime are only formed by going through hell with each other. That'd be something like Sandhurst. Or the Royal family.

And nothing can ever touch the experience of a bullet buzzing past your head. The truly close shaves: after a lifetime of Royal duties, they're the things Spares thirst for.

☆

Living with the Heir

Billy and I were both training to fly helicopters at RAF Shawbury in Shropshire, and because it seemed like a really brilliant idea, we both of us lived together in this cottage in Shawbury. Can you imagine? Two Royals living on top of each other in this tiny little house and not a flunkie to be seen. If the terrorists had got wind of it, that would have been one hell of a coup – in a single bang, they'd have bagged both the Heir AND the Spare. (And just made Uncle Andy's day – not to mention the whole goddamn year of Princess Beatrice. But that's another story.)

Six months we had of living with each other – and I can tell you that is one hell of a long time to be spending with your big brother, even when they're not the Heir.

So let me see now, as I remember it, the chores in our little house were fairly well divided. William did all the cooking, cleaning and washing-up, and I did all the telly-watching.

Stick it to the man! That is the job of the Spare – and do not forget it.

☆

Best. Christmas. Ever.

Not that Christmas at Sandringham isn't great. It is great. Surrounded by all your family. Your entire family plus assorted hangers-on. And hangovers.

You'll soon get used to the routine.

But that's the thing about Sandringham. The whole Christmas holiday is one long routine from start to finish. Nothing ever changes – and I don't doubt that when you're eighty, they'll still be doing things in exactly the same way that they were doing them when you were five years old.

Routines can be lovely. Cosy. Comforting. Get up. Bull shot. Kedgeree. Cherry brandy before church. Carols. Etcetera. Et-goddamn-cetera.

But after a while, Christmas gets bloody boring.

The same people, the same food, the same jokes – and, at least from Uncles Eddie and Andy, the exact same conversations that we had the year before and the year before that. (You'd have thought that I might have a lot in common with Eddie and Andy because we're all Spares. But somehow it's never clicked. But then again – these two guys did put the stuffy into Christmas stuffing.)

After Sandhurst, I went off to Bovington to train as an Armoured Reconnaissance Troop Leader. That's being the boss of a pack of four light tanks; three men per tank, eleven men at my beck and call.

The bosses asked for volunteers to be on duty over Christmas.

I volunteered like a shot. Bliss!

And that Christmas Day:

A little light brunch in the morning, a walk in the afternoon – no church, thank the Lord! - and turkey and a few sherbets in the evening; and all without once being hammered on the back by that bald buffoon Eddie; without being mooned over by those Princesses Beatrice and Eugenie (Princesses?? Do me a favour!); without having the Royal march to the church in the morning and without having to worshipfully listen to Granny's Christmas message, which may have become a part of Britain's Christmas tradition, but which is so stultifyingly dull it could curdle diesel oil.

Christmas is great. You'll love it.

You'll love it even more when you can do your own thing. But just like Sandhurst, you have to have spent many, many weeks at Sandringham before you appreciate life on the outside.

☆ ON FARTING

The Royals, including Her Majesty, adore farts and fruity language. What do I mean by 'fruity'? I mean four-letter words. Just so long as we're in private, then the conversation will always be liberally dosed with F-words and B-words. It is a small release from having to spend our time buttoned up as tight as corsets. Even your mum, Kate, still very new to this sort of thing, has started peppering her language with swear words. If you didn't do it, the whole thing would drive you mad.

It is the role of the Spare to be the court jester. Your language is expected to be far fruitier than anyone else's. You are leading the way.

You will also be expected to be... the Queen of the Farters.

What does this mean?

It means that whenever you are on public display, preferably conspicuous but distant, you will be expected to fart. Long and loud and smelly. **That's how we like it.**

The Buckingham Palace balcony is perfect. At least once a year we have to go through the shtick of the balcony gathering. It's the Windsors in their pomp, and it's all very grand, and the crowds love seeing us on display.

But if only they knew what was going on beneath the balustrade. We're all farting like wizards – a very small act of rebellion to keep our sanity. Look – we know this whole balcony thing is ridiculous. And we know we've got to do it.

So we knuckle under, and we smile and we wave, but secretly we are all farting and farting, to really show what we think of the whole farrago.

I remember once when Prince Phillip let fly an absolute ripper. The smell was so toxic that I almost gagged – and beside me I could hear Grandad howling with laughter, for that is what we are about: being poisoned by each other's farts and maintaining a stiff upper lip throughout.

So, my advice is learn how to fart. Long and loud and pungent. Eating lots of garlic will add to the beautiful aroma. It may sound weird but it is one of the few things that keeps us Royals happy.

I remember the first time my mum read me the story of *The Princess and the Pea*. This King and Queen live in a castle with their young son, and for some crazy reason the Prince has got it into his head that he wants to marry a '*real* Princess'. So various possible soulmates are shipped over to the castle, but none of them really cut it – because none of them are 'real Princesses'.

Then, one stormy night, there is a knocking at the front door, and this bedraggled woman is let in. She's soaked and she's pretty cold, but she is able to utter five important words: 'I am a *real* Princess.'

Well she might be a Princess and she might not, it's all very difficult to tell, so in the end the Queen has no option but to put the girl to the test. The Queen goes to one of the spare rooms, orders the bed to be stripped, and then places a small pea right in the middle of the bed. Twenty mattresses are then put on top of the pea – and the possible Princess is sent to bed.

'How did you sleep?' asks the Queen in the morning.

'Oh just terribly,' replies the girl. 'I'm black and blue from the horrible lumps in the bed.'

The Queen is thrilled – because now she knows for sure that this delicate creature must indeed be a *real* Princess.

When I heard the story, I said to my mum, 'Are you real princess?'

'Yes I am,' she says.

'So would a pea make you all black and blue?'

She laughed. Lovely laugh she had. 'It's just a fairytale.'

The story of *The Princess and the Pea* is indeed a fairytale.

Snow White – another fairytale.

Cinderella. Sleeping Beauty. Rumpelstiltskin. These are all fairy stories. They all have Princes and Princesses. The thing is though: these Princes and Princesses are ***fairytale* Royals**.

And the problem – at least for the likes of me – is that there are a lot of people out there who think these bloody stories are for real, and who are hoping, hoping, hoping that one day their damn Prince will come. Well that Prince isn't going to be coming any time soon – and even if he does come, it's probably just going to be me, the Spare, farting, swearing, drinking and generally behaving in a very un-Prince-like manner.

So let us just say that some people have quite high expectations about how Princes and Princesses ought to be behaving. I know it's ludicrous. But it's true.

And the reality is – always – going to fall substantially short of these expectations. I've come across women who imagine that all their problems will be over once this fairytale Prince (that'd be me) has come into their lives. They end up disappointed. Expectations crushed. And then they get angry. Why is this Prince behaving like just as much of an arse as every other guy?

I tell you now – these damnable fairy stories have not made life easy for us Royal Spares.

Be wary of absolutely anyone who starts talking about fairytales. Or who starts talking about knights on white chargers. Or who starts humming 'Some day my Prince will come'.

And if you do ever come across a man who starts going all misty-eyed at the mention of it all turning out happily ever after, then... proceed with extreme caution.

VERY USEFUL FACT #4

You should have seen us before we went out on the Thames for that pageant at the Diamond Jubilee. I was togged up as if I was about to schlep off to the North Pole. Vests. Thermals. Hand-warmers. The lot. At these showcase Royal events, you want to dress as if you're about to go out into an Arctic monsoon.
Hip flasks are useful.
Every chance you get, always have a pee.
There's nothing worse than having to small talk for two hours when you're desperate for the lavvy.

Oɴ ʙᴇɪɴɢ Gɪɴɢᴇʀ

I reckon I have heard every single ginger joke going.

I have also probably heard every single joke about where my ginger hair might have come from.

I'm cool about it.

Super-cool.

My hair may be ginger.

At least I've still got some.

TOP PRINCE HARRY JOKES: #7

The Duchess of Cambridge was asked in New Zealand whether she wanted her second baby to be a boy or a girl.

'I don't mind,' she said.

'Just so long as there's not a ginger hair in sight.'

Sᴛʀɪᴄᴛʟʏ Nᴏ Pʜᴏɴᴇs

My darling sister-in-law, your lovely mum, is just nuts about *Strictly Come Dancing*.

Loves it. Won't miss an episode. If she has to go out on a Saturday night, then woe betide anyone who tells her what's happened.

Never really understood the appeal of watching D-list luvvies dancing, but each to their own.

One Saturday night, Kate went along with a friend to see the show live. It was all very discreet – apart from the senior execs, no-one even knew she was there.

When she came back, she couldn't stop talking about the show, dropping all these names of people I'd never heard of, and talking about foxtrots and tangos like she'd been in a time warp back to the 1920s.

And then she mentioned something that I found very, very interesting.

Before the show, every single member of the audience – without exception – had to hand over their mobile phone. Until filming had ended, the phones were all kept in secure lockers.

Just in case, of course, someone's phone went off during the dancing. You know how it is – you tell everyone to turn off their phones, but there will always be at least a dozen dolts who leave their mobiles on.

Rather got me thinking.

If I were to rule the world, I'd make it a golden rule that if I am attending a party, then all guests' mobile phones will be impounded.

Couldn't care less about the phones going off.

What I could care about is being snapped making an arse of myself when I'm pissed.

I don't know why it is, but people will promise till they're blue in the face that they won't ever, ever be getting out their little pocket cameras – but then the very moment they see me in the nude with a pool cue in hand, the dollar signs start to appear in front of their eyes.

Naming the Monarch

When the monarch dies, the Heir Apparent can call themselves anything they like. They basically get to choose their name.

Take Edward VIII – your great-great-great-uncle. He was always David. I'd have thought it was quite cool to be Kind David The First.

But anyway – he picks the name Edward. Just another boring Edward.

Or your great-great-grandad, George VI. He was always Bertie. Decides to become George to accentuate how very English he is.

As the Royal Spare, I used to daydream about the names I might give myself if I ever got the top job.

Always rather liked the sound of **King Kevin The First.**

It's a nice little fantasy game to play when you are bored witless in church.

☆

THE ASTON MARTIN

What's my favourite car?

Aston Martin. Not a shadow of a doubt about it.

When we were kids, Billy and I were given an Aston Martin pedal-car. It was made by – guess who? – Aston Martin. They thought it would be a good stunt to give the car to the two young Princes.

One hell of a smart move.

Ever since, we've been obsessed with Aston Martins.

The thing was though, Billy, being two years older than me, always got to ride the thing. Once the bugger was in that car, you could never get him out of it.

The only way I ever got to have a ride was to get up early in the morning. I'd have an hour playing with the car and with all of Billy's toys before the Heir arrived on the scene.

It was my golden hour.

Start getting up early. You can start doing all the things that George won't let you.

☆

#

One of the buggers about being a Royal is that you have to spend a hell of a lot of time in church.

I HATE church.
☆

And I've had an absolute basinful of it.

At my prep school, Ludgrove, we had chapel in the morning and chapel in the evening. Every day without exception.

The list of hymns and psalms would be up on the wall, and I remember mentally ticking them off. I couldn't wait to get out of the place.

More chapel at Eton. A ton of chapel at Eton. In the morning, then prayers in the house at night and an extra big serving of Jesus on Sundays.

And even though I left school long ago, I still have to show my face at the occasional church service. The moment I step into the pew, all these school memories wash over me.

Billy, by the way, is also not a fan of church services. In one of my favourite stories about him, Billy excelled himself at Westminster Abbey. Uncle Andy was getting married to the Fergie-monster and for some reason they'd got it into their heads that four-year-old Billy would be the perfect page boy. He turned into His Royal Naughtiness!

Constant fidgeting, scratching, and sticking his revolting tongue out at anyone who looked at him. Attaboy, Billy! Grandmama was not amused.

So, you're going to be spending one hell of a lot of time in church.

You'll be doing yourself a huge favour if you learn to like it. (And if you do ever learn how to enjoy a church service, then let me know!)

☆

KNOWING YOU'RE A ROYAL

I must have been about four years old when I first realised I was... special. That I was in fact... a Prince.

That when it came to all these fairy stories that I was read before bedtime, I was in fact the star of the goddamn show!

Up until then, I suppose I'd thought that just about everyone else on earth lived in a huge house packed with flunkies; and that it was normal to be always accompanied by a butch guy in a suit with a pistol; and that there was nothing remotely strange about being hosed down by photographers every single time we set foot outside the house with my mum.

My parents had been pretty good at giving me as close as they could get to a normal upbringing. Palace staff were under specific orders to treat me and Billy just like any other snot-nosed kids. And if we didn't say our Pleases and Thank you's, they were more than entitled to tell us where to get off.

So, for the first few years of my life, I was certainly aware that I was living in this big house and in this busy social whirl, but did I have any idea that I was in fact one of these fairytale Princes?

Nope.

Not for a long, long time.

And then one day, I was on my little scooter in the gardens at Kensington Palace and the old man comes out with this army officer. The guy had red tabs on his collar, I remember, so he must have been quite high up the greasy pole.

The old man comes out, scratches me on the top of the head and says, 'Having a nice time?'

Then, the army officer who's got a brain the size of a shrunken pea gives me a full bow to the waist and says, **'Your Royal Highness.'**

I look at the man in total amazement and then burst out laughing.

Papa steps in – 'We don't have any of that here.' – but unfortunately a small seed has been planted in my head.

A little while later, I ferreted out the old man while he was in his office. He was sitting at his desk looking through some papers.

'Daddy,' I said. 'Why did that man call me Your Royal Highness?'

'Because he's a total wally.'

'What does it mean?'

'What does what mean?'

'What does Your Royal Highness mean?'

'It means that Major General will soon be looking

for a new job.'

'What does it mean?'

'What does what mean?'

'Your Royal Highness.'

'I have not got the faintest idea what you're on about, but I think you probably say it when you think someone's an idiot.'

'So he thinks I'm an idiot?'

The old man is screwing up a piece of paper between his fingers. He flicks it at me and it bounces off my head. 'Shall I tell him to join the club?'

I pause for a moment to digest all this. So this guy in a fancy uniform has just come into the garden, seen me on my bike and told me I'm an idiot?

'So why did he bow to me?'

'I've already told you,' says the old man. 'Because he's a wally who will soon be looking for a new job.'

'What's a wally?'

'A wally is a super-sized idiot.'

'Cool.'

I could see that I wasn't going to get much change out of the old man, so I stalked off out of the room – and found one of the flunkies.

'What's a Your Royal Highness?' I asked.

'Haven't got the faintest idea,' the man deadpans.

'Am I Your Royal Highness?'

'You're certainly a cheeky bugger.'

And onto the next member of the staff, one of the cooks: 'What's a Your Royal Highness?'

'A fat stuffed shirt, a piece of pond-life with less brains than a tadpole.'

'Am I Your Royal Highness?'

'You've got the makings of one – though you're not quite fat enough yet.'

And to the butler: 'What's a Your Royal Highness?'

He strokes his chin, as if pondering some matter of great moment. 'A Royal pain in the bum.'

'Am I a Your Royal Highness?'

'You most indubitably are.'

'A Royal Highness?'

'A Royal pain in the backside.'

I finally winkled out the truth from the boot-boy who came in to clean the shoes. In five minutes, the scales have fallen from my eyes: I'm not just a Your Royal Highness. I'm one of those bloody Princes that keeps on cropping up in all the fairy stories. **I am, in fact, a bit of a hero!**

For a little while, it quite goes to your head.

That's because you think it's all going to turn out just like the fairytales.

And then very soon you realise that for every Prince's perk, there is a corresponding inconvenience. A drawback. An unpleasant little detail that is working its way further and further up your nose and then down your oesophagus until it has eventually turned into the most almighty pain in the neck.

But quite good fun – those first few weeks when it ain't no joke. You are actually a 'Your Royal Highness' (and probably also an idiot with it).

Enjoy those few blissful weeks while you can! They will come to an end soon enough.

TOP PRINCE HARRY JOKES: #8
Prince Harry has blamed his antics on:
a broken home, family living off tax-payers,
growing up on estates and
time spent in institutions. ☆

ETON TRADITIONS - AND HOW TO CHANGE THEM

Like the Royal family, Eton also has its own traditions. I had a small part in changing one of them.

At the end of the summer term, the whole school has to take exams – either A-levels or GCSEs or the in-school exams.

For a long, long time, the results of the in-school exams would be read out to the entire year.

Picture the scene: all 250 boys in the year sitting in Eton's Farrer Theatre as the exam results are read out by the Lower Man.

Read out in descending order.

The Lower Man would start off with the first-placed boy, usually one of the scholars, and move on to the next and then the next.

Every boy in the room would be praying to hear their name – because the later your name came up, the lower your grade.

And ultimately, you would end up with the last boy's name. The boy who'd failed more exams than anyone else. This poor chap would usually be awarded 'A General Total Failure' and would henceforth forever be labelled 'The Thickest Boy In The Entire Goddamn Year'.

This had been the drill at Eton for several centuries.

The whole of the first year troop into the Farrer Theatre.

The results are read out.

And to his perpetual and everlasting shame, 'The Thickest Boy In The Entire Goddamn Year' is revealed.

But for some reason, when I took my first-year exams, this age-old tradition was abandoned. The thickies were no longer to be outed in public.

Instead, my exam results were revealed in the intimacy of my housemaster's study.

Andrew Gailey said I'd done jolly well.

For me.

(Incidentally, keeping exam results secret has since become standard at Eton – except when it came to my A-level results, when the doltish headmaster Tony Little well and truly let the cat out of the bag. I got a B and a D in my two A-levels, which was just about enough to get me into the army. But the year after I'd left Eton, the headman started gloating to the boys about the previous term's A-level results. And along the way just happened to mention that there'd only been ONE D-grade.)

So: Eton and the Royal family are equally mired in tradition, and most of the time it's lovely.

What can easily happen though is that you find yourself doing things, really stupid things, just because it's traditional.

You want to watch for that. Quite often there is in fact a better way to do something, don't let yourself be blinkered by tradition.

On Hacks ☆

Journalists – you either love 'em or you hate 'em.
Me?

Perhaps time for a little diplomacy here.

Plead the Fifth!

When the News of the Screws' 'Royal Editor' (what a title!) Clive Goodman got done for phone-hacking, they claimed that he was just this 'rogue operator'. A one-off. One very bad egg.

And then it turned out that, far from being a little one-man operation, phone-hacking was completely endemic across the whole of Fleet Street.

Hacks going to jail, right, left and centre.

Executives going to jail.

Know what happened in the Irish potato famine? A few potatoes were contaminated with potato blight – and very soon the entire potato crop had turned black and mouldy. Everything gone bad.

There was only one thing to do: get rid of the whole damn lot. Get rid of every last potato.

So am I suggesting that there is a direct correlation between Her Majesty's Press and a whole load of dud potato(-heads)? Am I saying that we should have done with every single one of those bottom-feeders and that they'd probably look best in the business end of a sausage-machine? Am I ever so slightly indicating that my world would be a much better, much more fragrant place if every single scum-sucking hack were consigned to the bottom of the Marianas Trench with a large cannonball chained to their legs?

Well you might think that. You probably will think that.

But it is not advisable to comment. You may loathe the scum-suckers. You may wish them all into the Seventh Circle of Hell. But to their faces, we are polite. We smile. We shake their hands.

And when you eat with them, which you will sometimes have to do, you will always dine with a very long spoon.

☆

The Snake and the Parrot

There is a pub near to my old man's house in the Cotswolds. In this pub they used to have a very exotic pet – remarkably similar in fact to that other equally exotic species, an HRH.

The pub is The Tunnel House, in Coates; it was the first pub where I drank alcohol, a half-pint of cider. The pub is in the middle of nowhere. You might have been there already.

It is much favoured by horny-handed agricultural students, and as a result, every single item has had to be screwed to the walls – pictures, brasses, nick-nacks, you name it. If it's not screwed down then it will be nicked.

There were two things that the students never quite managed to steal.

The first was a rather squawky green parrot that had the complete run of the pub. It had a perch on one of the walls, but it could fly wherever it wanted and would occasionally sit on the mantelpiece, warming its feathers above the fire.

The other exotic creature in this pub was a fourteen foot reticulated python, who spent almost all of its life caged in a glass pen by the bar.

He was sleeping the first time I saw him. The snake seemed to spend most of his life sleeping. I had a lot of sympathy for him, because he, of course, was the HRH of the animal world, perpetually stuck in this glass cage being mooned over by morons, and with every new day exactly identical to the last.

Every morning the door would be opened, and the snake could stretch himself and have a slither around the bar. He'd inspect the walls and the door and the benches, always looking for a way out. His entire life was the glass coop and the bar room, and I suppose the highlight of his day was when he got fed. They'd give him mice and rats and sometimes a chicken.

The parrot, meanwhile, liked nothing more than baiting the snake. Every day he'd fly down from his perch and would peck at the glass. Tap-tap-tap he'd go and the first few times the snake had been satisfyingly enraged, but after a few weeks, the snake just slept through it all.

Though just for old time's sake, the parrot continued to tap at the side of the snake coop.

One morning, the snake was asleep and the parrot was strutting around the side of the coop, tapping here and tapping there – just generally enjoying himself because he was free while this magnificent snake was stuck in prison.

The parrot continues to tap.

The snake continues to sleep.

The parrot is only a few inches away from the snake, separated by a sheet of plate glass.

Except there is no sheet of plate glass.

The door is wide open.

And the sleeping snake suddenly doesn't look quite so sleepy – in fact his eyes are wide open and he is coiled and ready to strike.

The python launches himself.

The parrot is swallowed completely whole.

And that, I'm pleased to say, was not just the end of the parrot, but the end of the reticulated python too. After he'd eaten the parrot, he was deemed too dangerous to stay in the pub, and shortly thereafter was moved to Bristol zoo where he joined all of the other snakes and had a very happy life, by all accounts, sireing an incredible number of snakelings and living to a ripe old age.

I often wonder how it will end for this particular Spare HRH. Am I destined to spend the rest of my days being gawped at by swivel-eyed muppets? Or will I one day behave so badly that my HRH title is forcibly removed and I am exiled from the Royal family?

Maybe…

Maybe if I managed to lay out one of the paparazzi scum-suckers, sorry – I mean 'esteemed members of Her Majesty's Press corps', and was up in court for causing Grievous Bodily Harm.

Now that might do it.

That might just do it.

No more HRH for me. No more Royal duties. Exiled forever from life in the goldfish bowl.

Please don't tempt me!

WHAT I WISH I'D KNOWN

VERY USEFUL FACT #5

When going out for a proper session that will involve
not just a great mixture of alcohol but also serious
quantities, it is advisable to line your stomach
beforehand. A tablespoon of virgin olive oil a half-
hour beforehand will be just perfect.
Means you'll be less likely to chunder in the night.
But you'll still have one hell of a hangover in the
morning.

The most Stupid thing ☆ I've Ever Done ☆

I've done many, many, many stupid things.

Though personally speaking, this one takes the biscuit.

I've said it before. I'll say it again. And again. You want to watch out for people recording you on their mobile phones. Everyone's at it these days. I can't set foot down the street without some mug getting out their phone.

It's not great. It is how it is.

When those mobile phones come out, then I am wary.

Very wary.

So therefore, it takes one very special sort of idiot to land himself in the shit on his own video.

I kind of thought that because it was me who was wielding the camera, then I'd be in the clear.

Seemingly not.

I'd been recording a number of army mates in Cyprus. We'd been out on exercise and were crashed out at the airport as we waited for the flight back home.

I'm just filming my Sandhurst buddies – and in amongst them is my pal Captain Ahmed Raza Khan, who I witlessly referred to in my running commentary as, 'our little Paki friend'.

What a **plonker!** What an **idiot!** What an utter **cock!**

It was bad enough saying it on camera – but for me, me, me to actually be wielding the camera...

Sometimes my idiocy amazes even me.

Later, on a night exercise, I was caught out yelling to another solder, 'F*** me! You look like a Raghead!'

I was given detention. The army sent me on a special 'diversity course' to make me more 'racially aware'.

There are no words.

You've got to be careful with your language.

Words like 'Paki' and 'Raghead' are always going to be a no-no.

But language changes. Words that were once acceptable can suddenly become highly offensive.

For instance: transsexual.

Used to be fine to call somebody a transsexual.

Not any more it ain't. Now they're transgender.

Look at how old Benedict Cumberbatch got himself into a ton of trouble by talking about 'coloured' actors rather than 'people of colour'.

It's a bloody minefield! Since a lot of what you're going to be saying is going to be recorded, then you have to be fully up to speed on the latest list of no-no words.

Oh yes. And one more thing.

There are lots of ways you can get yourself into trouble. But only a complete arse gets into trouble on their own damn video.

On Cameras ☆

Having been caught out so many times by muppets with mobile phones, you'd have thought that I'd have learned my lesson.

Well I've sort of learned my lesson – and that is, for every minute that I am out in public, I act as if I'm not just being filmed, but that that footage is going to instantly end up on YouTube.

I know that. These days, I do my best to remember that there are seemingly only two people on this earth who do not have a mobile phone. One of them is my granny and the other is her husband.

So when I'm out in public, no matter what the provocation, I try to behave myself. Not too much boozing. No hitting on girls. No mischief-making.

Except... even when you're in **'private'**, you've still got to be mighty careful about those bastards videoing you on their mobiles.

And that's pretty useful advice for not just you, but any Spare on earth. Getting up to mischief and general no good is fine. It's fantastic! It's brilliant. It's what we Spares can do while the Heirs are earnestly grinding away preparing themselves for the dull lives ahead of them.

Just don't – whatever you do – allow anyone to record you on their phone. Not that they'll use that footage today or tomorrow. But one day, when you're famous, when you're worth some money, when it might all be rather embarrassing... well that'll be the day when that video footage gets a slightly wider airing.

This one has caught me out time and time again. I think I'm in private. I think I can drink, have some fun. I think I can party and play pool with gorgeous girls in their bikinis and then – why the hell not? – play some naked pool too. I was born for it!

But at least once a year there's some juicy new video footage of me that ends up going viral. Sometimes it's from people's mobiles. Sometimes it's from the CCTV cameras. Sometimes it's even from the hotel lifts. Who knows where the camera is going to be, but somewhere there's going to be a camera.

And in ten years' time it'll be even worse!

So, unless you're with your very close family or your very oldest friends, then you want to assume that you're being videoed or recorded.

And for everyone else out there, all those other Spares, IF you're doing something that is slightly bending the rules, or is illegal, or perhaps distasteful... then just make sure that there are no cameras around!

And if, while you're making mischief, you do just happen to catch someone with a camera, then confiscate it. Smash it. Throw it in the sea. Teach these bastards a lesson.

I'm not saying don't misbehave. That's what we Spares were born to do. But if you do do it... well just make sure you're not caught on camera.

Otherwise, as my great-granny used to say, you'll be in for a 'skelpit leatherin'.

THE EXCEPTION TO THE RULE:

THE TOOTH AND THE ☆ WHOLE TOOTH ☆

Of course, there's an exception to the rule. While I advise you to be wary of others trying to get a pic of you, by all means, try and get pics of others...

Your dear old dad has got this completely undeserved reputation for being a squeaky-clean Prince who is for ever thinking about his Royal duties, and who has never once brought shame upon the House of Windsor.

I, on the other hand, am famous for being reckless and stupid. I am the Prince who has to be closely monitored at all times to stop me making a dick of myself. Fair enough. I have committed a good number of howlers over the years. Big bruv Billy on the other hand...

I have no idea what sort of pact he's signed with the devil, but it must be one hell of a deal that satan cooked up for Billy – because although my big bruv has committed all manner of horrors, he's never once been caught.

Not once!

I know I shouldn't be telling tales out of school.
It's wrong.
It's inappropriate.
It's unseemly for senior members of the Royal family to start blabbing secrets.

Do I care?

Well let me ask you: do I look as if I care?

Herewith: one of the most cracking stories you will ever hear about Billy, but which never even came close to getting into the papers.

I therefore feel it is my duty – both my Royal duty and my fraternal duty – to make amends. Besides – where's the fun in life if you can't occasionally land the Heir in the shit?

It was about a week before your brother George was born, and so the entire world was in a very high state of alert. There's a new Heir on the way, folks, and Prince Harry is about to be bumped from his slot as the nation's 'Official Spare'. Boo-bloody-hoo!

Be that as it may, Billy was still adamant that he wanted to go to a wedding up at Alnwick Castle. That's the place that doubled for Hogwarts in the Harry Potter films.

Your mum Kate was a little bit snotty about him leaving her all alone – 'what will happen if the contractions start?' – but Billy soft-soaped her into giving him a pink ticket. That's what he always does, the bastard – just switches on those soulful puppy-dog eyes, and the next thing you've lost your nerve and you've folded.

I was also at the wedding, so I guess I pretty much had a ringside seat. And let me just say: I haven't enjoyed a wedding even half so much as that wedding in Alnwick.

We go through all the usual rigmarole in the church. I am counting the seconds till I get out of the place. The groom kisses the bride, loving smiles all around, the music strikes up and Prince Harry is history! I'm out that church so fast I'm practically holding onto the groom's coat-tails.

We drink Champagne, we take our seats at the wedding breakfast – and, what a surprise, the Royal Spare is surrounded by a clutch of beautiful single women. One of the big perks of being a Spare is that you are (perceived to be) one of Britain's most eligible bachelors – which roughly translates to meaning that at weddings, dinner parties, formal ho-downs and such like, the hosts make an especial effort to sit you next to the cream of the totty! Phwoooarrr! Not all bad being the Spare, I can tell you. Probably not as much fun when you're married. Not quite sure. I'll keep you posted on that one.

Anyway. We drink, we dance, we drink some more, and I chat uproariously to the two women I'm sat next to – and seeing as neither of them have ever met a Prince before, they hang on my every word. I could be reading out the telephone directory and they'd still be mesmerised.

There might have been fireworks that night, there might not have been fireworks that night – haven't got a clue as all these weddings tend to meld into one.

New husband and wife retire to their honeymoon suite.

And what, meanwhile, of Prince Billy?

As my great-grandmother was very fond of saying, Billy was becoming **'fusionless with drink'**.

He was utterly skunked and by 3am he was getting skunkier.

There was some horseplay. Alright – we were fighting. Not throwing punches, but a number of us were wrestling. Proper army wrestling, that is, like you'd see in the officers' mess. You're not necessarily trying to deck the guy. But you'd certainly like to cause him a bit of pain.

Suddenly there's this squeal of pain. I turn and look. **And instantly burst out laughing.**
The bugger's had his front tooth knocked out!
There's a bit of blood round his chops, his tooth's on the floor, and he's got this dazed look on his face like Alfred E. Neuman, the gap-toothed kid on the front cover of *Mad* magazine.

Well I know what I've got to do – and I'm doing it, I'm doing it.
I've got to get that picture. I want the picture of the toothless Heir with his torn waistcoat and claret on his white shirt.
Finally – finally! – I've got the bastard bending!
It's a picture that's going to go right round the world, a picture to dog Billy for the rest of his days.
It would have been worth an absolute fortune - six figures at least.
I'd have given it away for nothing, just for the sheer pleasure of landing Billy right up to his Royal neck in it.

I've got my phone out by now, but the thing is switched off. Turn the thing on, but it's taking ages to connect, and then you know how it is, I'm frantically trying to tap in my password, but I keep on muffing it, and things are absolutely desperate now, as I can see that this brilliant window of opportunity is fast shutting on me: Billy is being escorted to the bathroom to clean himself up, and then, Howl! Howl! Howl! I've missed it!

The next day, it is a very tight-lipped Billy who is heading back south to his wife in London; by the afternoon the tooth has been fixed and by the next day, Billy's simpering gob is back to its pearly-white best, and yet again he's got away with it. A few days later he's holding Baby George and his butter-wouldn't-melt-in-my-mouth smile is being flashed all the way round the world.

And I'm left there thinking: if only I'd got that damn picture.

If only.

Have you ever seen a bulldog strutting down the street, tail in the air, balls swinging in the breeze?

From the front these bulldogs look just great. All tough and rippling with muscle. But from behind – with their balls in their hairless ball-bags – they look ridiculous.

Ahhh... did anyone happen to mention playing pool in the nude? I mean – you may have thought that a bulldog looks pretty ridiculous, but you ought to take a look at a naked guy when he's bending over a pool table.

Skin burned.

Legs akimbo.

Balls a' swingin'.

Though as it turned out, looking like a prize pillock was the very least of my nude-pool problems.

Let me tell you how it all started.

I'd been asked to Las Vegas for a party, a wet and wild party at the MGM Grand. They were so keen to have me that they were even going to stump up an exclusive chalet for me and a few pals. They imagined that having a Prince there might add some much-needed **class** to the occasion.

Seeing as I was soon going to be shipped out to Afghanistan, and seeing as there was going to be an absolute army of beautiful, scantily clad women there, not to mention enough booze to float a battleship, I accepted the invite.

Off we fly to this hell-hot desert which has somehow been turned into a gambling Mecca, and then, come the next morning, the party starts in earnest.

I would guess there were well over 2,000 people at the MGM for the Wet Republic pool party – and every one of them fully intent on getting off their skulls on booze. By tea-time, there was probably more piss in the pool than there was water. Couples openly shagging by the poolside! (At least give me credit for not doing that!)

I put on my shades. I put on my red beach shorts and my white Panama. Oh – and now that I think of it, I also put on my necklace. Mustn't forget the necklace!

We move on from the poolside to the casino bar, and from the casino bar to the VIP chalet, and in the

VIP chalet there happens to be a pool table. That's what you get when you fork out £1,000 a night. (Not that it was me who was doing any of the forking.)

At this stage things get a little hazy.

I can remember that we carried on drinking.

I can remember that we started playing pool.

And I suppose, I guess, that at some stage some idiot – perhaps even me – may have suggested playing strip-pool. **Why, why, why?** Anyway – strip-pool it was, and thank God I'd got that necklace on because otherwise I really would have been stark bollock naked.

And then, what a surprise, a girl wants to make a phone call, and just happens to take a picture, and then the picture is sent to her boyfriend, and then...

Away we go.

For some rotten low-life it was jackpot time.

And for me: just a little embarrassing. **Ho-hum.**

Funny how things turn out though. In the long-term, it did my cred no end of good. Even years afterwards, when I was out meeting and greeting, kids were giving me much more respect than I ever deserved.

That had nothing whatsoever to do with me being a Prince – and everything to do with those naked Vegas snaps.

And my advice is?

When you've got your kecks off, make sure no-one's got a camera.

Obviously.

But also, remember that bulldog swaggering down the street! **Whatever you do – don't play nude pool.**

Not even George Clooney could carry it off! I very much doubt that the truly scrumptious Taylor Swift could carry it off. And therefore... it's unlikely that you'll be able to carry it off. (Though a crown might help, but leave that one to Prince George.)

♔
TOP PRINCE HARRY JOKES: #9
Seeing Prince Harry's bollocks has changed my life.
I'll never eat a Scotch egg again.

ON HOLIDAYS

Some multi-millionaires try to worm their way into your affections by giving money to your favourite charity. As the patron, you will have to sit next to them at the next gala ball. (Another slice of rubber chicken? Yes please.)

There are other ways that rich people will try to become your friend.

They will ask you to parties.

They will be on committees with which you are involved: Olympic committees, World Cup committees, football committees, you-name-it-they'll-be-on-it committees.

And then there is the holiday invite.

Watch out for these ones.

This is what happened before I knew any better.

A fat boring control freak who also by chance happened to be a billionaire asked me on holiday.

No expense spared! Bring along some friends! Private jets all the way, unlimited booze, any food I wanted, any

TOP PRINCE HARRY JOKES: #10

Can we therefore conclude from the photographs that Prince Harry is not a very good strip-billiards player?

amusement whatsoever, it was all ours for the asking, and all conducted in the most complete privacy.

Of course we did have to spend a couple of days with the billionaire before he left us to it. Didn't like him. He was in his sixties – wouldn't have looked at any of us young pups if I wasn't a Royal.

After two days, off goes our new billionaire friend to wherever the hell he wants to go and the party continues. We're glad to see the back of him.

Two nights before we're about to leave, it's raining and we're all inside, sitting around the fire in this most lavish room with a wall of windows that overlooks the Atlantic. The room has had a lot of money spent on it, but apart from the view, it is the tackiest place I've ever been in. As you well know, from the moment we are born, we are surrounded by the finest things that money can buy. I know tat when I see it. And trust me, this place is filled up with rich kitsch, as if our billionaire friend wants to show off his trophies to the next willing magazine. Paintings crammed on the walls, nick-nacks fighting for space on the mantelpiece, tables festooned with gold tat, and chairs that were eye-poppingly expensive but damn uncomfortable to sit in.

We are drinking our way through our host's most expensive bottles of Champagne. He'd told us to help ourselves – and we were.

A cork pings into a hideous nick-nack on the mantelpiece. It is a seagull in flight made of gold and precious jewels – and as the cork hits it, one of the jewels pops out.

I may have been half-skunked, but I could still recognise a teeny-tiny camera when I saw one.

Time, perhaps, to call in my bodyguard.

Turned out the jewels on this nick-nack were nothing but paste.

Turned out there were quite a few spy cameras in this expensive holiday spot - in fact probably more spy cameras than in the entire *Big Brother* household.

Never heard from the billionaire again – so I never did find out if he was going to blackmail us, or if he was just some pervy voyeur.

But these days I am more circumspect about accepting invitations: invitations for dinner, invitations for the weekend, and, in particular, invitations to go off on an everything-paid-for holiday. Occasionally, very occasionally, you might come across a free lunch, but there is certainly no such thing as a free holiday.

On Speeches ☆

I was about eighteen the first time I had to give a speech. It was a charity bash – just saying thank you to the fundraisers and good luck to the kids.

This was a speech that I had really prepared for.

Every word of it written out. I'd read it so many times that I had practically memorised the thing.

The old man had also given me some coaching. 'Just imagine they've all got their trousers down and they're having a dump,' he says. Thanks, Pops.

160

Billy also has some sterling advice. 'You just want to relax,' he says. **'R-e-e-e-l-a-x!** It's no big deal.'

And of course the old man is right and Billy is right. When you're giving a speech, all you have to do is imagine that every audience member is sitting on the can, and then you can r-e-e-e-e-lax. Really r-e-e-e-e-lax.

Except it's all a little different when it's for real. When the MC says, 'Give it up for Prince Harry!' The lights are on you and the cameras are on you and you stumble over to the podium and instead of staring out at an audience with their trousers round their legs, they, all of them, look fully clothed, thoroughly clothed, and I don't know why, but that first time, the audience put me in mind of a herd of zombies who would like nothing more than to chew me limb from limb.

I stuttered through the speech.

And when I had to do the next speech, I stuttered through that one as well.

Nerves! Anxiety! We are talking Prince Bertie in *The King's Speech!*

After about a year, I was on the very verge of a full-blown panic attack.

I'm just about to step onto the stage. Huge audience. I am shaking from head to toe.

A friend comes over. 'Break a leg, Harry,' he says – and then he sees that I've gone completely white.

'I'd rather break a leg than face that lot,' I said.

He pulls out a hip flask. 'Have a slug of this.'

It was cheap whisky, bloody raw and bloody rough. I had a shot and I had another, and after I'd stopped hacking, I could feel the fire spread through my veins – and by the time I was up at the podium, the audience didn't just have their trousers round their ankles, they were stark bollock naked.

Speeches are always nervy affairs. It helps if you've got the speech all taped, it helps if you can imagine the audience on the can and it'll help, also, if you can just re-e-e-e-lax. But nothing's going to help quite so much as taking a stiff tot before you go on stage. Just a tot, mind, because otherwise...

Otherwise bad things can happen. (Can you imagine the headlines? Pissed Harry Slurs His Speech.) But of all the many Royal gaffes to be notched up on the Royal score-sheet, this is one that I haven't committed.

Yet.   ☆

☆

CHRISTMAS PRESENTS

The story goes that when the Duchess of Fergie first joined the Royal family for Christmas at Sandringham, she went to the most immense care buying everyone presents. She spent weeks and weeks on picking just the right gifts for her in-laws, rather expensive gifts, but if you're giving something to Her Majesty The Queen, then Jamie Oliver's latest Christmas cookbook isn't really going to cut it. Tasteful presents for her brothers-in-law, for her sisters-in-law, and presents, also, for all the nieces, nephews and assorted cousins and second cousins twice-removed who creep out of the woodwork at that festive time of year.

She'd really gone to a lot of work. And expense. Had been most thoughtful.

162

Total and utter embarrassment.

Humiliation. Uncle Andy might at least have tipped her the wink.

That is not the way we do things in the Royal family. When it comes to Christmas presents, you're allowed to spend ten quid, top whack.

Better yet, you make the present yourself. A pretty little picture, suitably scatological if it's for your great-grandad or any of your great-uncles (or your uncle or parents, come to that). A picture of a corgi having a slash against a Christmas tree; Rudolph the reindeer pooing against Santa's sleigh; the Christ-child peeing from his infant crib. Those will all go down an absolute storm.

But whatever you do, don't spend a bean on the presents. Very frugal, the Royals are – especially when it comes to buying presents.

Phone-Hacking

I'd been to a lap-dancing club.

Quite discreet. I'd told Billy about it, and the next thing he'd left a message on my voicemail – squawking away on the phone, pretending to be a pissed-off Chelsy.

I was pretty surprised when that story ended up in the newspapers. I mean, apart from me and Billy, who else would have known about it?

Couldn't trust anyone in those days. We thought that one of our closest friends, one of the inner circle, was flogging stuff to the Press.

When in fact for at least three or four years our phones had been hacked by journalists, mainly from the News of the Screws though I'll bet the hacks from the other papers were all at it.

It was a story about Billy that was their undoing. Just a tiny little item about him injuring his knee during a kick-about. And after that, we knew our phones were being hacked. And after that, some of the hackers went to jail. And after that, one of Britain's oldest newspapers went to the wall.

Our phones aren't hacked any more. **Probably.**

And our emails aren't being hacked either. **Probably.**

But if I've got anything important to say to somebody, then I like to do it face to face. Love doing it face to face. (And in ten years' time, I'll learn that, along with everything else, the buggers have bloody bugged Kensington Palace. Ho-hum.)

In Conclusion: The Heir

And so, as I come to the end of this little *Spare Heir Handbook*, I find that, for some quite unaccountable reason, I have failed to mention something of great import.

Maybe it just slipped my mind. Maybe I wanted to leave it to last.

Can't think why I haven't touched on it before.

But anyway – for whatever reason, I have failed to address this important, this most crucial of topics, and now, in my own very modest way, it is time for me to make amends.

In truth, I suppose I've left it until last because I know that this is one of those oh-so-taboo subjects which

164

genteel people are just not meant to discuss – least of all Royal Spares when they're talking about their big brothers.

Still, sometimes you just have to get something off your chest.

If you don't get it off your chest, then it starts to rankle. Fester. Eats you up. Know what I mean?

And this is something that I've been meaning to get off my chest for some time.

Now I do appreciate that this is not normally a fit subject for polite conversation.

I am also aware that this might seem a little bit unfair, a little bit unnecessary, a little bit, I don't know, MEAN.

Frankly, I have no real idea about how to go about addressing this oh-so-delicate subject.

In fact, I don't know if there is any easy way to say it.

But anyway... **a Spare's gotta do what a Spare's gotta do.**

You see, the truth is, well, that Prince Billy, Heir to the Throne and all the rest of it... well he's a bit of a baldy isn't he? Within ten years, he'll be as bald as an egg. Bald as the shining bonnet on a waxed Aston Martin. Bald as a Belisha beacon.

His shining bonce will be so smooth that you could skate on it.

His pasty white pate will have such a gleam on it that if ever the Bell Rock Lighthouse ran out of juice, you could just stick Billy up there, bald head aglow, and the ships would see him all the way from the other side of the Channel! (Even in the fog!)

Now I'm not saying that Billy's bald head is shiny – but let us just say that the Ferrari chief executive was recently in touch, just to ascertain whether Billy could give them tips on how to get some extra shine on the latest super-car.

I can't tell you how awful it's all been for Billy.

I mean not that he was ever really a looker – but he wasn't a total minger either.

And now he has barely a hair left on his head.

Very touchy about it, he was, for a long, long time.

I tried – tried so hard – to point out the benefits of being bald.

No need to spend a fortune on shampoo, conditioner and hair gel, not to mention all those very (very) expensive hair-loss unguents on which he used to spend an absolute fortune.

No more wasting your time having to wash your hair.

Or visit the hairdressers.

No need ever, ever again to use a swim cap.

Or a brush.

Or a comb.

Or a mirror.

No necessity, ever again, to have to deal with great piles of fan-mail from dribbling women aquiver with lust at His Royal Gorgeousness.

No more dandruff. Ever.

No need for blow-dries, no need to have a hissy-fit when it's wet and the rain is mussing up your gorgeous tresses.

Hmmm…

And oh yes! No need, ever, ever, again, to have to fret about losing your bloody hair! Once you've lost your hair, then the worst is over. There's nothing left to fear! You've lost it! You're a baldy – and you better bloody get used to it, ya soor-faced slaphead!

Just trying to accentuate the positive.

Just trying, in my usual blunt, honest, Sparely way, to be helpful. But I think it would also be fair to admit that, very, very occasionally, I may have given Billy a wee bit of chafing about his Supreme Baldness. Just the odd bit of fraternal banter.

What has this meant in practice?   ☆

I will tell you!

In Billy's case, HRH Chrome-Dome was losing his hair in his early twenties, and by the time he was thirty, the writing was well and truly on the wall: when he finally got to the throne, the old bugger was going to be the baldest King in Christendom! (Even Prince Albert of Monaco has got a bit of tufty hair around his ears, but not our Billy. When he gets to be King, he'll have more hair on his arsehole than he does on his entire skull.)

And it was my humble lot to let HRH Baldicoot know that all his hair was falling out – and this I have tried to do to the very best of my limited abilities.

For instance:

Star Trek comes on the TV. Well – really only one thing to say isn't there? 'To Baldly Go Where No Man Has Gone Before…'

Or, while watching some nature programme: 'Tell me Billy – what is America's national animal? Could it be the… Bald Eagle?'

Or: 'Billy – you don't have something to write with?

Maybe a Bald Point pen?'

Or… telling His Serene Baldiness that whenever I knock the top off a bald – sorry, boiled – egg, I think of him.

Or… games of snooker, pool, bar billiards, or pretty much anything that involves a ball that is both shiny and hairless. It is the Spare's job, nay his Royal DUTY, to remind the Heir that his head bears an uncanny resemblance to said billiard ball, and are they perhaps cousins?

Whereupon?

I mean why should Billy's bald head be of any concern to me when, even though I'm a ginger, I do also happen to be in possession of that very rare thing – to wit, A FULL HEAD OF HAIR!

So let me spell it out.

Heirs have their weaknesses.

It is the job of the Spare – ginger or otherwise – to winkle out those weaknesses.

And then tease the Heir. Mercilessly and without surcease.

The more they hate it, the more you've got to dish it out to them.

As already mentioned, the Heir spends his entire life surrounded by brown-nosers, sycophants and grease-balls.

It's your job, as the Spare, to be the antidote to this ocean of slime.

You are the sour to the sweet.

You are the sharp, shitty stick that is poked – frequently – into the Heir's eye.

So: you see that weakness.
Seize it.
Never let it go.
**That is the main role of HRH Spareness.
And you're gonna love it – I know you will! Me?
Frankly, I think it's the best thing on earth about
being the Spare!**

Some home truths for you my dear...

Some 205 square miles of prime English land
– valued at over £750 million.
An annual profit of over £19 million.
That'd be the Duchy of Cornwall.
A prime piece of British real estate.
All the loot goes to the Prince of Wales,
dontcha know.
And therefore…
It'll be a long, long time before His Royal
Spareness is on the receiving end of any of
that cash.

. . . .

Earl of Chester.
Duke of Cornwall.
Duke of Rothesay.
Earl of Carrick.
Baron of Renfrew.
Lord of the Isles.
Prince and Great Steward of Scotland.
And there's one more, what is it now –
oh yes! Prince of Wales.
These are all titles that go to the Heir.
Spares don't get to see these titles any time soon.

It's got 775 rooms – including 19 state rooms (the big 'uns), 52 Royal and guest bedrooms (the nice 'uns), 188 staff bedrooms (the not so nice 'uns) and 78 bathrooms (nice and not so nice 'uns).
That'd be Buckingham Palace.
Quite a nice pad, really. Very convenient because it's bang in the middle of London.
The Spare gets to know this place quite well.
Just won't ever live there…

· ·

Some 7,000 paintings. Over 40,000 watercolours; a whole load more prints. And – oh yes, and an absolute blizzard of stamps, millions of the buggers. That'd be the Royal Collection and the Royal Stamp Collection (as collected by the terrifying George V). Cracking good stuff – well some of it. Most of it's pretty boring actually. Not that this will be of any concern to you, because as the Spare your pretty little head will not be troubled whatsoever by such things.
So not your problem!

Over 50,000 acres. Grouse moors. Loads of deer.
All the other gubbins that you'd expect on a big
Highland estate. And – oh yes, a damn big house.
That'd be Balmoral.
Interestingly, Balmoral is not Crown property, but
belongs to the Royals.
Won't make much odds either way if you're the
Spare; Spares do not ever get their hands on the
Balmoral Estate.

. . . .

The Koh-i-Noor diamond – that's a big diamond.
About the size of a plum.
And the Cullinan diamonds, a pair of the buggers,
they're pretty big too.
And the Black Prince's ruby. He's a big 'un – about
the size of a ping pong ball.
And then there are thousands more diamonds, not
to mention pearls, rubies, emeralds and sapphires,
all of them stuck together by the Queen's jewellers,
Garrard & Co. of London's fair city.
These are the baubles that make up the Crown
Jewels – crowns, sceptres, orbs, swords, rings,
spoons and bracelets.
You certainly won't get to wear 'em.
Tell you the truth, it's pretty unusual for the Spare
even to be allowed to touch 'em.
Just like with all the other Royal goodies, the Spare
can look all they want, but they're never allowed to
touch.

We hope you enjoyed Prince Harry's helpful tips for the Spare Heir, and any other back-up siblings out there.

For more Royal musings, follow Bill @thespare_heir